GRAVE MATTERS

A Demon Trappers Novella

Other Books
by Jana Oliver

Briar Rose
Young Adult novel
Macmillan Children's Books (U.K.)

Tangled Souls
Paranormal Romance

Time Rovers Series
Time Travel/Alternate History Romance
Sojourn
Virtual Evil
Madman's Dance

The Demon Trappers Series
Young Adult series
U.S. (U.K.)

The Demon Trapper's Daughter (Forsaken)
Soul Thief (Forbidden)
Forgiven
Foretold

Grave Matters

A Demon Trappers Novella

Jana Oliver

 Nevermore Books

Published by
MageSpell LLC
P.O. Box 1126
Norcross, GA 30091

Grave Matters
A Demon Trappers® Novella
ISBN: 978-0-9704490-8-5

To my readers...
who love Riley and Beck
as much as I do.

Acknowledgements

I owe a *huge* thank you to my critique partners (Berta Platas, Michele Roper, Carla Fredd and Maureen Hardegree) who cajoled, wrangled and frog-marched me through this novella, confident that when I finished it would be worthy of my readers.

A big hug and some fermented spirits to Tyra Burton, who did a quick proofread of the manuscript while on vacation, no less. True friends are always there for you even when they could have been eating beignets.

And finally my gratitude to the city of Edinburgh, who knows it's wise to preserve history rather than burying it.

"It is better to conquer yourself
than to win a thousand battles.
Then the victory is yours.
It cannot be taken from you,
not by angels or by demons,
heaven or hell."

— Buddha

Chapter One

Late October, 2018
Atlanta

Riley Blackthorne compared her seat number to the row numbers above the seats. Confused, she shot a look behind her, toward the area of the airplane designated for Coach Class. She should be back there, right?

There has to be a mistake.

But it appeared there wasn't, so she kept working her way forward in the section located between steerage and Business Class. Apparently Grand Master Stewart had upgraded her seat to something called World Traveler Plus.

How cool is that?

When the woman behind her delivered a not so subtle nudge with her purse, Riley shuffled forward, continuing to check numbers against the boarding pass clutched tightly in her hand. There was another nudge to her left kidney.

"Look, if you're in a hurry, go around me, okay?" Riley said. *It's not like you're going to leave any earlier.*

The statuesque woman narrowed her eyes and did just that, ensuring that her wheeled suitcase rolled over Riley's shoe, leaving a black mark on the leather.

Sighing, Riley dropped into her assigned seat, which was definitely more comfortable than she'd expected. Knowing that clutching her backpack to her chest made her look like a dork, she stuffed it under the seat in front of her. After chucking off her coat, she gave a quick look at her seatmate, a graying, middle-aged businessman. His computer screen displayed a multi-colored graph as he tapped away on the keyboard.

"Hi," she said, unsure of seatmate etiquette. It was only the third time she'd flown and the earlier trips had been when she was really young.

The guy gave a nod in her direction and went back to his work. *At least he's not going to talk me to death.*

After wetting a tissue with spit and cleaning off her shoe, she checked out the other passengers as they settled in for the flight. Most appeared to be business people. An exception was the young couple who sat across from her, all laughter and smiles. Riley couldn't help but notice the woman's sparkly ring.

"Pretty ring," Riley said.

"We just got engaged," the woman replied, her voice light and airy.

"Congratulations!"

Maybe that'll be me on the way home. That was her greatest wish.

Riley had been waiting for this trip ever since her Demon Trapper boyfriend had left Atlanta right after Labor Day. Now that Denver Beck was halfway through his grand master training in Scotland, it was time for a visit. Their mentor, Grand Master Angus Stewart, had arranged it all. He'd even paid for the plane ticket, because there would have been no way Riley could have afforded this trip. But, like all things with Stewart, she suspected he had other reasons for her to go to Edinburgh besides seeing Beck and celebrating her birthday. No doubt, she'd figure those out once she got there.

In fact, Stewart was supposed to be traveling with her, but he'd acquired a bad case of pneumonia which had kept him in his bed. In the year she'd known him, the older man had never gotten sick. Despite his grumbling and complaining – in between coughing fits – he knew better than to travel no matter how eager he was to visit his homeland once again.

Riley's nerves kicked in and she found it hard not to fidget. Even if she was only a few days short of turning eighteen, this was her first overseas trip. Luckily Beck would be waiting for her. She checked her watch – eight hours and twenty-seven minutes from now she'd be in his arms.

The memory of their last kiss surfaced now, along with how she'd cried when they'd said goodbye. How he'd looked like he'd wanted to as well, but had held it together. Riley twisted the ring on her right hand, the one he'd given her last spring. It was his grandmother's wedding ring, an old silver band with an ivy pattern carved into it. On a sudden impulse, she pulled it off and slid it on her left ring finger and then smiled because the ring looked good, like it belonged there. Worrying someone might have seen that strange maneuver, she moved it back and then nestled her hands together in her lap.

I miss you so much.

The couple near her was laughing again, reminding her of the good times she'd missed, how much Beck had woven himself into her life and her heart. Over the two months he'd been gone they'd talked once a week, and she'd sent him care packages and pictures of his rabbit so he'd wouldn't feel like she and Rennie had forgotten him.

Like we ever could.

In a candid moment, Beck had admitted the grand master training was difficult. "Damned hard" was the way he'd put it. A native of South Georgia, he'd had a rough childhood and his reading skills weren't the strongest, so that had made the studying difficult. Still, he'd been doing okay. As he'd put it, "They haven't tossed my ass to the curb yet."

So far Beck had beaten the odds. To become a grand master was a rarity in itself; he'd killed a Fallen angel – no mean feat – and survived what might have been a one-way trip to Hell. Now he was learning how to balance good and evil in this world. It was a life-changing responsibility, but she knew he'd do fine. Still, a part of her was worried. How would she fit into his new life? Would things still be good between them like they had been before he'd left? Or would he find he no longer needed her?

Riley's cell phone pinged and she welcomed the distraction. It was a text from her best friend Peter, who was majorly jealous she was headed to Scotland without him.

HAVE FUN! WATCH OUT FOR THOSE HAGGIS. THEY BITE.

Riley chuckled to herself. Ever since she'd told him she was going to Edinburgh, there'd been a steady stream of haggis jokes. He'd claimed all sorts of outlandish things about the Scottish food, including that it was actually a hairy beast that ran wild in the Highlands.

They traded texts for a time and then she sent a message to Beck knowing he wouldn't reply – it was well after two in the morning over there.

Right before it came time to power down the phone she received a reply.

LOVE U, PRINCESS. SEE U SOON.

You are awake. Which meant he really was looking forward to seeing her.

LOVE YOU TOO.

On impulse, Riley kissed the phone, then noted her seatmate's bemused expression.

"Really fond of your cell phone?" he asked in an American accent.

"No, really fond of my boyfriend," she said. "He's meeting me in Edinburgh."

"Is he Scottish?" the man asked.

"No, he's from Atlanta. He's ... studying there."

"What is he studying?"

"World history."

Which really wasn't a lie except that all that history related to the endless war between Heaven and Hell.

The citizens of Atlanta certainly knew about demons – they'd had their fill of Hellspawn-related catastrophes earlier in the year, and the body count that went with each of those encounters. They knew about Holy Water and how it was used and that there were different kinds of demon trappers, ranging from the apprentices to journeymen and onto the master trappers. However, most folks did not know about the *grand* masters of the International Demon

Trappers Guild, and she didn't feel at liberty to explain exactly what Beck was up to.

After powering down her phone, Riley kept her eyes closed during takeoff, her fingers gripping the seat tightly. Her ears popped repeatedly but once the plane was in the air, she heaved a sigh of relief.

After supper, Riley retrieved the book she'd bought in the terminal bookshop, hoping the hours would pass quickly. Fortunately, the novel sucked her right in, an inventive story about a young woman named Kate who wielded magic and kicked some major monster butt in a totally screwed-up 2040's Atlanta. To Riley's amusement, the hero, a shape shifter lion dude, sounded like a total hunk.

Just like Beck.

Riley woke up in time for breakfast, her neck stiff. Apparently she'd been more tired than she'd imagined, but that wasn't surprising as the last six months had been hectic: her early graduation from high school, the steady stream of new apprentices to train, study time for the single college class she attended, plus taking care of Beck's house and bunny since he'd left for Scotland. Being busy was good – if she had more time to think she would have missed him so much more.

During the few lull times Stewart had her studying for the Master Demon Trapper's exam. She was already a journeyman and master was the next step. He'd warned her it was unlikely that the National Demon Trappers Guild would let her take the exam in the next year or so, but eventually their skittishness about Paul Blackthorne and his daughter would fade. Skittishness that was righteous in many ways.

She'd already killed an Archfiend, one of the requirements to take the next step to master level. The rest should be just paperwork, but she and Stewart knew it wouldn't be that easy. In many ways, Riley had followed in her father's footsteps since he'd sold his soul to Hell to keep her safe. After she'd taken a Fallen angel as her first lover, she'd given up her soul to prevent Atlanta from being destroyed.

Then there were her meetings with Lucifer and the Vatican's Demon Hunters. Even though she had regained her soul from Hell – just like her dad – all of that drama meant the trapper dudes at the national level regarded Blackthornes with frank suspicion, if not disgust.

In all honesty, Riley couldn't blame them. She just had too much baggage, and a lot of it wasn't road worthy.

It doesn't matter how long it takes, I'll be a master someday.

It was the only way she could repay her dad's sacrifice.

~ - ~ - ~

Immigration and customs in Edinburgh went quickly and, after a trip to the restroom to tidy up so she could look her best for Beck, Riley found her way to the International Arrivals Hall. The instant she turned on her phone it pinged, which meant the international dialing plan Stewart had arranged was working just fine.

Unfortunately, the message was from Beck and it was bad news, an unwelcome change of plans.

WAS SICK THIS AM. BETTER NOW. DAVID BRENNAN PICKING U UP.

The text was an hour old, but that didn't blunt Riley's muttered swear word.

What is it with the guys getting sick? Beck only got ill if a demon scratched him up.

A second message quickly followed the first.

SEE U @ 9 @ HOTEL. LOVE U.

Shaking her head, Riley pushed forward toward the Arrivals Area. Maybe this was for the best; she could check in, get a quick shower and a nap. That way she'd be in good shape for when Beck arrived. Or least that's the lie she told herself to cover her supreme disappointment. Sighing with deep regret, Riley walked further into the Arrivals area. After some searching around she spied a man holding a sign with her name on it. Beck hadn't given her a description, but who else would know she was arriving this afternoon?

Brennan was in his early thirties, with a thin build and dark hair and eyes. From what Beck had told her, he was sort of an all-purpose gopher for the grand masters. Since it was more than a four and half hour roundtrip from the master's headquarters to Edinburgh and back, Brennan had pretty much blown the day picking up Beck's girlfriend.

Wonder what he thinks of that.

Something made her hesitate, then Riley shook off her nerves. Walking up to the man, she cleared her throat. "Hi. Are you David Brennan?"

He blinked, studying her. "Ah, yes I am." His accent was upper crust English, which she hadn't expected.

"Oh good. I'm Riley. Is Beck okay now? He said he'd been sick."

"Ah … yes, he's better. Some sort of food poisoning." Brennan took hold of her suitcase and waved her forward. "Come along."

Adjusting her backpack, she followed him. She'd expected a bit more friendliness, but maybe the guy was tired or something. It didn't matter anyway – in a few hours Beck would meet her at the hotel and it'd all be good. Right now, nothing else mattered.

It was just before dusk when they exited the terminal. Riley took her first long inhalation of Scottish air and found it more crisp and clean than in Atlanta. Fall had definitely taken hold here, and in response she buttoned up her coat.

Brennan wove them through the parking lot, past various vehicles until he stopped at a red sedan where he popped the trunk lid and put her single piece of luggage inside. There was a large canvas bag in there as well, and a folded piece of steel-gray cloth. As he slammed the trunk lid, the driver's side door opened and a woman stepped out wearing a thick blue sweater and a pair of jeans. Her pale blond hair was pulled back in a messy bun. She looked in her late thirties and her makeup certainly wasn't concealing the dark circles under her eyes.

Beck hadn't mentioned Brennan would have anyone with him.

"Hi. I'm Riley," she said.

"Bess," the woman replied.

Riley didn't reply, caution ruling her curiosity. There was no guarantee this person knew a thing about the grand masters or Beck.

Brennan stepped in. "Bess is ... a friend of mine. After we leave you at the hotel, we're going for dinner."

Which meant Riley wasn't quite as much a burden as she'd thought.

"Oh, that sounds good. Glad to meet you, Bess."

When Brennan insisted Riley take the passenger seat, she buckled herself in. "This is my first time in Scotland," she announced, still astounded she was now in a different country.

"I'm sure it will be an interesting visit," Bess replied, as she slipped back into the driver's seat. At Riley's puzzled look, she explained, "I live in Edinburgh. I know my way around better."

That made sense.

Brennan climbed in the back and checked his mobile phone, his brows furrowed in concentration as he typed out a text message.

Riley turned her attention to the scenery as it went from airport to countryside. Though it was growing darker, in the headlights she caught a road sign that said A8. All the while her mind screamed that they were driving on the *wrong* side of the road and likely to die at any moment. As they looped through a roundabout, she finally relaxed.

She thought of asking her babysitters a few questions, but they didn't appear to be in the mood to chat. That was okay, in a few short hours she could put all those questions to Beck.

He had the itinerary all drawn up; after a few days of sightseeing in Edinburgh, he was taking her to the Highlands and the manor house where the grand masters had their headquarters. Apparently, it was quite the place, since Beck wasn't easily impressed.

Her cell phone pinged and she pulled it out of her coat pocket. It was Beck and that generated an instant smile.

BRENNAN RUNNING LATE. BE THERE IN 30 MIN. STAY PUT.

She shook her head because this text had to be old.

NO SWEAT. IN THE CAR & HEADED TO THE HOTEL.

"Who is that?" Brennan asked from the back seat.

His rude question jarred her. "Huh? Just Beck telling me you were going to be late."

Her phone rang and she wasn't surprised to see it was her guy, probably just wanting to hear her voice. "That's him now."

Brennan swore. "Too soon."

"What?" Riley asked as she went to answer the call.

A second later she was pulled back against the headrest, Brennan's muscular arm encircling her throat. As Riley clawed to free herself, her phone went flying. The sting of magic pricked her skin as he began to chant a spell.

Unable to cry out, the magic tunneled her vision, and then the world went dark.

Chapter Two

As Denver Beck fled down the three flights of stairs to the main floor of the two-century old manor house, he nearly collided with the housekeeper. He didn't slow long enough to apologize, worry driving him forward as he jogged along the hallway. Once he reached the grand master's door, he pounded on it. While he waited for a reply, Beck paced, muscles knotted and heart racing.

"Come!" a voice called out.

A phone rang as Beck hurried inside, causing him to come to an abrupt halt. Grand Master Trevor MacTavish waved him toward a chair as he took the call, but Beck remained upright, too nervous to sit.

His superior was about Angus Stewart's age, early sixties, with world-weary blue eyes, his silver hair tied back in a ponytail. His muscles were sculpted as if formed by solid steel.

While MacTavish worked through the call, Beck's eyes rose to the massive stained glass window behind the master's desk, a work of art that captured the moment Lucifer had been booted out of Heaven. Behind the plummeting figure were banks of clouds and stars, with the light pouring down from above. Whoever had created the window had caught Lucifer's likeness perfectly, which meant the artist must have met him in person.

Poor bastard.

Every time Beck saw that image he winced, a visceral reminder that no one was above falling from grace, not even a grand master. No doubt that was why it was here.

MacTavish hung up the phone, eyed Beck for a moment then frowned. "Tell me what's troublin' ya, lad," the man said, his

Scottish accent lighter than most.

Beck began to pace again, it was that or bellow his frustration. "I was textin' back and forth with Riley, tellin' her that Brennan was runnin' a little late. She says she's already in the car with him, but when I tried to call her there was no answer. So I called Brennan. He just got to the airport and Riley's nowhere to be seen."

Beck didn't wait for a reply. "Somethin's wrong, I can feel in my gut."

"Then we'll trust that feelin'. That's the kind of intuition that keeps us alive."

The grand master thumbed his cell phone. "Brennan, it's MacTavish. Have ya located the Blackthorne girl yet?" He frowned at the answer. Then the frown deepened. "What?" he said. "No, don't come back here. Walk around. She has ta be there. This might just be a misunderstandin', but we canna take any chances."

He ended the call and set the phone aside.

"Well?" Beck demanded.

MacTavish shook his head. "She's not where she should be."

Beck sank into the closest chair, his mind tumbling over and over.

This was his fault; he should have been there to meet her. He'd planned to, and then he'd been ill most of the day, throwing up. A stomach bug he thought, though that wasn't normal for him. When Brennan had offered to pick her up to give him time to recover, it seemed like a great plan – Beck would take the train down to Edinburgh later and meet Riley at the hotel about nine. Then they'd make up for all the months they'd been apart.

Grand Master MacTavish was on his phone again, this time speaking to someone in airport security. He relayed his request and ended the call.

"They're gonna review the security tapes."

"They don't know what she looks like," Beck said.

"That's why I'm sending them a photo of Riley from our files," MacTavish replied, his fingers tapping across his computer keyboard.

The minutes felt like days as they waited. Beck tried to call

Riley again and got her voice mail. *Where is she?*

He jumped when the grand master's phone trilled.

"MacTavish." The frown was back again. "Yer sure? What about the parkin' lot? Aye, please check those tapes as well. Thank ya." He hung up. "The security folks say Riley was picked up by a man who was holdin' a sign with her name on it. He was tall and thin and dark haired."

"Ah, shit. If he had a sign, she would have thought it was Brennan," Beck muttering, skimming a hand through his hair in agitation. "I should have told her what he looked like, but I never thought..." *That anyone would try to mess with her here.* "Why would anyone want her, besides me, that is."

"Time will tell if this is a straightforward kidnappin' for ransom or somethin' else."

"I'm not rich, so askin' for money is a waste of time," Beck countered. Which meant this was probably something entirely different, and that didn't make him feel any better. He surged to his feet. "I need to borrow one of the cars. I have to get to Edinburgh as soon as possible."

"I'll drive ya myself," MacTavish said as he rose from behind the desk.

"I swear, if she's hurt, I'll kill the sonovabitch who did this," Beck warned, his fists knotted.

"Aye, lad. That's just one of the reasons I'm comin' with ya."

~ ~ ~ ~ ~

A chill brought Riley back to consciousness, the sort that began deep in her bones and then leached out into her skin. Grass tickled her face and her entire left side ached from being in a cramped position for too long. But how long had it been?

Riley took inventory as best she could: her arms were tied in front of her and a blindfold covered her eyes. She tried to swallow against the thick phlegm in her throat while the scent of crisp air assaulted her nose. A slight breeze blew through her hair and traffic noises echoed in the distance. She was in a city. Edinburgh? They'd been driving in that direction when Brennan had ambushed her.

Her temper stirred. *What the hell is all this about?*

The faint tug of necromantic magic skittered across her skin and it made her shiver. Riley knew that all too well, experienced it firsthand when she and her summoner friend, Mortimer Alexander, had called up a demon in an Atlanta cemetery.

"We have to perform the ritual now," a male voice insisted.

Brennan.

Why would he do this? He has to know the grand masters will go ballistic.

"Robbie, this is kidnapping," another man protested, voice quavering with worry, his accent hailing from somewhere south of the Scottish border.

Robbie? Beck had said that Brennan's first name was Dave.

Riley had just taken this guy's word that he was Brennan.

I'm so stupid.

"No one said anything about committing a crime," a third voice complained, a female, but it wasn't Bess, the woman in the car. "You said the girl would come to us willingly."

"It doesn't matter," Robbie said.

"It will when the police come after us," the woman replied.

The numbness in Riley's left arm left her no choice but to move and try to restore circulation. The instant she did, a shoe nudged her in the knee.

"You're awake. Sit up," Robbie ordered.

So much for stealth intelligence gathering.

It took some effort to pull herself upright, but Riley got it done. As the blood coursed back into the arm, she winced in discomfort. When she reached for the blindfold she was warned against removing it.

"Behave yourself, and when this is over you can go free," Robbie warned.

Like I believe that.

They had committed a felony, and Riley suspected the Scottish cops wouldn't be any more forgiving about that than the police in Atlanta.

"If this is about money," she began.

"It's not," Robbie replied.

"How did you know I was coming to Scotland?"

"Be quiet."

Since Robbie and Bess had known when she'd be arriving at the airport, that meant someone within the grand masters organization had ratted her out. That wasn't a comforting thought.

In response, Riley's lungs began to constrict, the harbinger of a panic attack. *Not now!* She focused on taking careful, measured breaths, refusing to give into her body's desire to freak out. By now Beck would be tearing the city apart trying to find her, and he wouldn't be on his own; the grand masters would take her disappearance personally.

Thinking of her guy helped calm her fears, got her mind back in the game. With her breathing under control, it was time to figure out what was really going on.

"What's up with this, guys?" she asked, hating that she couldn't see them, couldn't read their facial expressions.

"All we need is some of your blood for a spell," was Robbie's curt reply.

Blood?

Even her friend Mort didn't use that in his incantations, and neither had Lord Ozymandias, the most senior summoner in Atlanta. Using blood was old school, creepy even.

Bound the way she was there was no way Riley could get free and screaming for help wasn't likely to do her much good or they'd have gagged her. Her only chance was to get them to believe she was fine with all this.

"I can help you," she offered.

There was silence.

"I'm serious. I've ... studied with a necromancer. I know how spells work."

The other male took the bait. "If she can help us—" he began.

"That's enough, Callan," Robbie said.

"Come on, take off the blindfold, will you?" Riley urged.

There was a long pause and then, to her surprise, the cloth was removed. Riley's guess had been correct; they were in a graveyard and it appeared to be very old one, with a line of weathered crypts stretching along a tall stone wall. Some were sealed, others missing a roof or door.

Four figures stood a short distance way, two in pale gray robes, their faces obscured by hoods. Bess was present, but in still in her street clothes, which meant she probably wasn't a summoner. Robbie was near her, his hood back and his robe a darker steel grey. That must have been the fabric Riley saw in the car's trunk.

Summoners indicated their magical ability by the color of their robes – the more prowess, the darker the fabric. That the robes were all shades of grey told her kidnappers were just past novice grade.

Riley zeroed on a despondent Bess. "Why am I here?"

"I'm sorry." She shot a frown at Robbie. "I didn't know he was going to do that to you."

"Same here," the other woman said, flipping back her hood to reveal curly blond hair. She was in her mid-twenties and stood closer to Callan than the others. His girlfriend perhaps?

None of this made sense. The closest gravestones were dated from the eighteen hundreds. Necromancers usually called up the recently deceased, not people who had been dead since the Civil War.

"So what's really going on?" Riley pressed.

"My daughter ... is dying," Bess said, choking up. "She's only five and the doctors don't ... know why. We have to summon an angel, to cure her."

That wasn't as crazy as it sounded – Riley's ex-boyfriend Simon Adler was currently wandering the globe in search of his lost faith because of just such a miracle.

Still, this felt weird: a desperate mother, three low grade necros and some wild ass idea that they can control one of Heaven's big boys? It was a recipe for disaster, on feathered wings.

It was time to let them know just what they could be facing.

"You're right, angels can cure people, but they can be *really* touchy," Riley replied. "If you can call one up – and that's a really big if – there is *no guarantee* that it won't be pissed and kill us all."

"No! They're not like that," Bess insisted, blinking back tears. "They're loving and kind. An angel will heal Mavis, I know it."

The woman's desperation was so thick Riley was surprised it didn't suffocate her.

Riley turned her attention to Robbie, hoping to get through to him. "It's good that you're trying to help, but you're out of your league here. Angels are serious business and you're just junior summoners. This won't go well, I promise."

"It will go just fine," Robbie replied, but she could see beads of sweat on his forehead now, despite the chilly night air.

"Why do you need my blood? Angels don't need that. That's dark magic."

"We're using your blood because Hell owns your soul," Robbie said solemnly. "What better bait than one who is damned?"

"Damned?" Riley replied. "No way."

The price to reclaim her soul had been far too high – it'd taken the death of someone she'd really cared about to get it back. She thought of showing them Heaven's mark, the crown embedded in the palm of her left hand, but somehow she doubted it would change their minds. "I swear, my soul is my own."

He ignored her, extracting a piece of parchment from under his robe. "If you interfere, I will cut your throat and then we'll have plenty of blood. Do you understand?"

A gasp came from the others, along with immediate protests. It appeared that this dude was working on a different wavelength than the other three. But why was that? What did he get out of this?

Street cred. A lower level necro who summons an angel would suddenly rate a lot more respect from his betters. Might even jump him a few grades up in the darker robe scale.

Robbie was the threat here, not Bess or the other two.

"Get her blood," he ordered.

Callan knelt next to her, the ceremonial knife in his shaking hand. "I'm sorry," he said, his sad eyes meeting hers. "But we really need to do this if Bess' daughter is going to make it."

"This isn't going to work. Your magic isn't strong enough to hold an angel."

"Callan?" Robbie nudged. "Get it done."

"Don't worry," Callan murmured, "I won't let anything happen to you, I swear."

Riley didn't bother to fight, but looked away as the knife met her arm, gritting her teeth as the slice caused her blood to trickle into the chalice. Once it was over, Callan took the time to bind the wound with a length of gauze and adhesive tape.

"Thank you," she said. He nodded, his face pale now. Before he stood, he pointedly laid the bloodied knife within her reach. Then he gave her nod and stepped back.

Her stomach queasy and her arm throbbing, Riley desperately tried to remember everything she knew about angels. Unfortunately, most of it wasn't comforting; they were scary and deadly creatures, even the ones who called Heaven their home.

Riley began to slowly move her bound hands nearer to the knife. Robbie wasn't paying attention to her now, too busy setting the protective circle around himself and the others. She continued to pull the knife closer in little tugs. It wouldn't protect her against a pissed-off angel, but if she could free herself, she might be able to escape.

Only a bit more...

The magical circle popped into existence, but it was weaker than Riley would have expected. Before she could point that out, Robbie began to intone a steady stream of Latin, with the other necros holding their breath. Bess was pale as moonlight, her hands clenched in front of her.

As the summoning spell wove around them, Riley studied it like an ancient manuscript, cherry-picking through the Latin, noting what words she understood. There should have been more brightness in the various phrases if you were summoning one of Heaven's winged messengers. More praise and awe, less ... darkness.

Riley looked up at the others, wondering if they'd noticed that darker undercurrent. Callan's eyes were wider now and he gave her a panicked expression. Apparently she wasn't the only one wondering just what kind of incantation was being woven.

The moment Robbie poured her blood onto the ground, the spell turned sinister, the words purely malevolent, not the kind you'd use to call up one of Heaven's creatures.

Oh, God!

Robbie was summoning a demon.

Chapter Three

The drive to Edinburgh had been two and a half hours of hell. About an hour in, Beck had stopped calling Riley's cell phone, knowing it was useless. It'd taken all of his control not to hurl his own phone out of the car window in frustration.

What if she's hurt? What if she's... ?

"Don't go borrowin' trouble, lad," MacTavish said, as if he'd read his mind.

"Why the hell not? Anythin' could be happenin to her and–"

"I know it's hard," the older man conceded.

Beck nodded, his fists knotted again. He wanted to kick and bellow and beat up the whole world until Riley was safe in his arms.

"We'll find her," the older man said softly.

"God, I hope so," Beck whispered. He'd planned it out to be perfect and now everything had gone wrong. He'd looked forward to her visit as much as Riley had, eager to see her, touch her. Love her again.

She has to be scared, but she'll be smart and fight back. Riley was a survivor. That was why he still held hope.

MacTavish's cell phone rang and the conversation lasted a number of minutes. Beck tried to read something from his expression, but the man had what Riley called a stone face.

"Good or bad news?" Beck asked as his superior ended the call.

"Mixed," MacTavish admitted. "They located the car on the airport security video and traced it a Robert Kinross. He's an English businessman who has been living in Scotland for the last decade. He's also a summoner."

"A necromancer?" That Beck hadn't expected and it took his worries in a whole new direction. "This isn't about money, then."

"I'd say that's exactly the case," MacTavish replied. "Not everyone believes yer lass' soul is her own."

"Do you?" Beck asked before he could stop himself.

MacTavish hesitated. "I trust Stewart's judgment on that. If he says she's on the straight and narrow, I believe him. If I didn't, she wouldn't be allowed anywhere near the manor."

Beck knew the International Guild and the grand masters kept close track of his girlfriend. It had begun even before they were dating, when Riley's dad, Paul, had given his soul to Hell. Stewart had been making regular reports to the head office here in Scotland, and while that hadn't surprised Beck, the depth of those updates had. Now he knew it'd all gone into their archives, so that in hundred years another fresh-faced grand master trainee could read exactly what had happened in Atlanta during the hellish spring of 2018.

MacTavish continued his ruminations. "Riley's experiences with Heaven and Hell, with the angels and the demons, could prove too encitin' for some. Perhaps her kidnappers believe she can help them gain power through her relationship with Lucifer."

"She doesn't have one. At least not anymore," Beck grumbled.

"Aye, but do they know that?"

The traffic noticeably slowed, making Beck grind his teeth. At least they were on the outskirts of Edinburgh now.

"I heard ya were ill this mornin'," his superior said. "How so?"

"I got sick right after breakfast. Throwin' up. Don't know why. Felt like crap for about six hours or so and then it cleared up."

"No lingerin' effects?"

"A little light-headed. I've been drinkin' lots of water," Beck replied, indicating a bottle sticking out of his backpack. "When I knew I wouldn't make it to the airport, Brennan went instead."

MacTavish gave him a sidelong glance. "Did ya ask him ta do that, or did he make the offer?"

"Ah ... he offered. I was too busy barfin' to ask him myself. I figured it was no big deal. I'd get a couple hours of sleep then head down and meet up with Riley."

"This is the first time ya've been sick since ya arrived, am I right?"

Beck nodded. "Well, except that cold I caught on the plane on the way over here."

"Just as I thought." MacTavish turned off the motorway and began to thread his way down the winding streets, trying to avoid the tourists.

"Where are we headed?" Beck asked.

"Police station. Thought it the best place ta be while they search for that car. They'll keep us in the loop."

That surprised Beck. "You and the cops work together over here?"

"Aye. What about Atlanta?"

"They're pretty good," he allowed. "It's the mayor's office that's the pain in the ass."

"Politicians," MacTavish snorted. "I swear Lucifer created those vermin just ta give us a wee taste of Hell."

Beck couldn't argue with that.

His superior's phone lit up again. "Understood, thank ya." MacTavish ended the call. "They found the car at Edinburgh Waverely."

"The train station would have a security video, right?"

"Aye. They're reviewin' it now. But why take her ta such a public place? There'd be too much of an opportunity for her ta try ta escape."

MacTavish had a point, and it was one that made Beck's blood chill. "Do ya think they took her somewhere else and just ditched the car so we'd think she was on the train?"

"Possibly."

"Then where is she? What's happenin' to her?" he asked, though he knew his companion had no answers.

What if I never see her alive again?

~ ~ ~ ~

Even before Riley could call out a warning there was a dark crack of energy and something popped into existence fifteen feet above them. The form was shrouded in a white cloak, like a silky chrysalis awaiting the birth of a gigantic butterfly.

"It came!" Bess cried as fat tears ran down her face. "Oh, thank God!" She shot a glance over at Callan. "See, it really came!"

Elaine stared upward in wonder. When Callan took her hand she smiled over at him.

"See, I told you it would work," she said.

Robbie was frowning, displeased.

You jerk, you knew what that spell was for. Now he was wondering why his demon hadn't appeared. Apparently he didn't realize that certain higher-level Hellspawn could mimic just about anything.

The shroud unwound and floated away in the breeze revealing eyes of chilly Arctic blue and black hair that flowed around the being's stern face. Just like you'd expect with one of Heaven's own.

No, not quite.

Riley knew angels, she'd stood toe-to-toe with the Archangel Michael while bargaining to save mankind from Armageddon.

This didn't feel like one of them.

Slowly the wings extended, gray-white feathers with dark black tips.

Riley remembered those markings all too well. She'd last seen them on a Fallen angel.

"Guys ... this isn't an–"

"Bow down before me," the figure commanded. "Worship me!"

Callan, Bess and Elaine instantly fell to their knees. Only Robbie remained standing. He shot Riley a dark look, a warning to hold her silence.

You set these people up.

Until she was free, there wasn't much she could do. Her fingers curved around the knife handle and hastily sawed on the ropes.

"My daughter," Bess began, trembling.

The being stared down at her, cocking its head as if it was reading her thoughts. "Swear your soul to me and she will be made well."

"My soul?"

The ropes severed and Riley shook them off. She shifted the knife to her left hand and then allowed the fingers of her right to curve around a small piece of broken headstone. She rose, unsteady.

"This is *not* one of Heaven's angels," she said. "They don't ask for your soul. Only demons and Fallen do that."

"Silence!" the figure said, turning those seething blue eyes upon her.

Riley could feel it picking around the edges of her mind, but it couldn't get a firm grip. Ever since Ori had trained her how to kill Hellspawn, she'd been able to block out their mind games, keep them from messing with her head.

"No, you're wrong. You have to be," Bess said, though her voice was uncertain. She began to tremble, bright tears reforming. "My daughter..."

"It *is* an angel," Elaine insisted.

"Are you sure?" Callan asked.

"I can feel it filling me with white light."

Oh boy.

Riley shifted her attention to the thing above them. "Come on down and touch holy ground. Then we'll know you're for real."

"I do not heed the orders of mortals," it replied.

"I know, but if you're really an angel, you'll do it so you can help this lady's daughter get well."

The being didn't move.

"She's right. Why isn't it down here with us? It should be able to rest on sanctified ground," Callan said as he rose from his knees.

Riley's fingers tightened on the piece of headstone. "We're waiting," she called out.

"Give me your soul and you will be spared," the thing promised, skewering her with those unholy eyes.

"Been there, done that, not going there again," Riley muttered. *I hope I'm not wrong.*

She launched the piece of gravestone into the air, and when it struck a wing, a brilliant spark erupted. The being snarled in response.

"My God, what have you done?" Bess cried. "Now it won't help us!"

As if on command, the illusion began to shred, beginning

with that wing. Feathers smoked and vanished, leaving behind an expanse of leathery skin that culminated in a wicked set of claws.

"Oh damn," Riley muttered. "An Archfiend."

Just once I wish I was wrong.

The demon was a little over six feet in height, its curiously domed head displaying three pairs of eyes, each of which shown with crimson fury. It wore only a loin cloth and the sword it carried was curved, blazing with black fire. A few months before, Riley had killed one of its brethren and wounded another. Back then she'd had the help of a Fallen angel; this time there was no Ori, and she was on her own.

"Why do you necros keep doing this kind of crap?" she demanded, rounding on Robbie. "Don't you ever learn?"

He ignored her, stepping closer to the edge of the glowing circle, but careful to remain inside. "I have summoned you, Hellspawn. You are my servant! You will obey me!"

"You *knew* you were calling up a demon?" Callan said. "What the hell were you thinking?"

"It is mine to command," Robbie replied tersely. "It will heal the child if I order it."

"I obey no mortal," the fiend said, its massive wings sending downdrafts that swirled dust around them. Then it smiled, a sight that made Riley's blood turn to ice.

The protective circle around the others began to warp, its light fading like a dying sun. With a distinctive snap, it vanished.

"The ward!" Elaine cried. "Put it back up!"

Robbie didn't bother – with a vicious oath, he took off at a run, leaving the others behind.

"Don't!" Riley called out, but the man kept moving. Robbie made it only a short distance before the demon cut him down with its blazing sword, his screams dying on his lips as his body fell in two distinct pieces.

Riley's stomach roiled and she looked away, the man's twitching torso resurrecting gruesome memories she'd tried hard to bury. She grabbed Bess and shoved her behind a large headstone as the other two scrambled to find their own cover.

Callan began to creep among the gravestones, working his way toward one of the open crypts. It was a smart move – if they could get inside the structure, the demon couldn't grab onto them without risking one of its wings touching sanctified ground.

"Come on!" he called out, waving to them. "Over here." Despite Riley's urging, Bess refused to move, her body locked in terror.

"Come on!" he repeated, stepping away from the crypt to beckon to them, heedlessly exposing himself.

"Callan, look out!" Elaine called out.

The demon's sword missed him, but one of its talons did not. It caught him in the back, impaling him as the Archfiend rose in the air with a triumphant roar.

"Callan!" Elaine cried.

"Give me your soul and I will spare you," the Archfiend demanded.

Callan shook his head, his face contorted in agony. "No."

"Give me your soul!" it bellowed.

"Never," Callan cried out.

Before Riley could find a way to intervene, the demon sent him sailing over the stone wall on the far side of the graveyard. Callan's scream slit the night. It cut off abruptly.

Elaine began to wail, beating the ground with her fists.

"Give me your souls," the demon said, winging back toward them. "Or ... give me Blackthorne's daughter and you will all go free."

Riley knew it was lying. Their only hope was for the others to get to safety, then it would be up to her to take care of the thing. She couldn't let an Archfiend loose on Edinburgh.

She shook Bess, hard. "Get inside the crypt and stay there, do you understand? Take Elaine with you."

Bess nodded numbly.

Then, after sucking in a deep breath, Riley uttered a quick prayer and stood. Carrying only the knife, she stepped out into the open, making herself the target. Even though Ori had trained her how to kill these things, he'd provided her with a cool angelic sword to do it.

Not this time around.

"Blackthorne's daughter," the Archfiend called out as it hovered above her, marking time with its wings. Its voice was thick and gravelly, probably from inhaling purgatory's sulfuric fumes for eternity.

"Go back to Hell, demon. You have no place here." Of course, there was no chance this thing would be so awestruck by her presence it'd head right back to the fiery pits in complete terror.

"I am here until those who summoned me are my servants. Or dead."

"Wow, color me surprised."

"If you agree to serve me, I will spare the others."

Archfiends weren't usually this chatty as playing fair wasn't in their nature.

Why is it stalling?

"Elaine, no!" Bess called out.

Riley spun around a second before the woman swung at her, a broken brick in hand. As it was, it just brushed past Riley's skull.

"You got Callan killed, you bitch! Your blood summoned it!" Elaine said, swinging again and missing. "It just wants you, not us!"

Riley wrestled the brick away and tossed it aside. "Don't listen to the thing! It's lying to you."

"Run, little one, run away," the demon said.

"No!" Riley cried, but before she could wrestle Elaine to the ground, the woman took off. Instead of heading for the crypt, and safety, she fled down the footpath, following in Robbie's doomed steps.

"Elaine!" Bess called out. "Come back!"

As the demon scooped her up, there was a sickening crack and Elaine hung limply in its claws, her neck broken. The fiend howled in rage at having lost a potential servant, and with only a few beats of its wings the body was unceremoniously dropped over the wall to join Callan in death.

"Dammit!" Riley raged. She didn't really care what had happened to Robbie – he probably deserved his fate – but now two others were dead.

Over the pounding of her heart she heard the sound of sirens, which meant cops might be headed here. They had no weapons to take down such a demon and they'd die just as quickly as the magical folks had, or find themselves Hell's servants for eternity.

It was up to her to kill the thing. But how?

Holy ground was her best weapon, but how could she get the Archfiend to touch one of the monuments or the earth? She studied the graveyard's landscape in the pale moonlight. *There has to be some way for this to work.* All she needed was enough open ground to get a good head start and…

"I will release your father's soul," the fiend offered.

Did this thing think she was stupid?

"Nice try, but he's in Heaven."

A snarl. "What of the Fallen, the one named Ori? Do you not wish to see him again? Have him touch you as he once did?"

Her fury began to burn hotter. "Ori is dead. And he's not in Hell either, so don't bother lying to me. Just shut up, dumbass!"

The instant she used the "d" word she thought of Beck and she felt her courage rise. She could hear his voice so plainly now.

All or nothin', girl.

"All or nothing," she repeated.

Riley took off across the open ground, not bothering to hide. Above her she heard the flap of wings as the demon grew closer. Dodging around headstones, she tried hard not to trip, her goal a statue, one close by a tall turret-like structure. The heat off the demon's sword grew closer as she sprinted the final distance.

The fiend snarled again, furious that its mind games weren't working. "I shall rip your flesh from your bones and feed upon you. Your blood I will drink."

"Yeah, yeah," she murmured, leaping over a headstone.

Right before Riley reached the base of the monument, the creature swooped close and slapped at her with a wing, causing her to fall. As she struggled to rise, it hung above her, creating a whirlwind with its wings. It raised its flaming sword to carve her in half.

At the last moment, she regained her feet, grabbed up her knife and took off. When she reached the monument, she scaled the steps, gaining height, until she reached the statue's legs. Her breath ragged, she waited for the demon to fly closer.

"Hey! What are you waiting for? Christmas?" she taunted.

The Archfiend snarled and swooped in, trying to knock her free of the statue. As the massive wing drew near, the talon already bloodstained, Riley leapt toward it. It was insane thing to do, but as she slammed against the wing, she slashed at the tendons with the knife. With a bellow the demon grabbed onto her arm with a claw and begin to rise.

She stabbed again and this time, the demon twisted in mid-air, shrieking in fury as black blood rained down. Its damaged wing could no longer support its weight and it sank lower. As it tried to compensate, the fiend veered too close to the turret and clipped it, causing holy white light to sear into like a beacon. For a moment it seemed caught, like a fly in a spider's web, twisting and crying out.

Fearing it would free itself, Riley frantically clawed her way up the fiend and threw herself against the wing, pinning it against the turret. The pain mounted as white-hot energy roared through her limbs, her joints, her muscles and into her back. She swore she could hear her blood sizzle in her veins.

In a final bid for freedom, the demon raked at her with a claw, pushing her free. Riley hit the earth, hard. Fighting for breath, she struggled to her knees and crawled toward the monument. The fiend fell, landing in a heap, its cries deafening as the sacred soil purged itself of the evil. Writhing like a giant burning moth in its death throes, it rolled over and over and finally came to rest some ten feet away.

Riley leaned back against the statue, black blood caking on her face. Her head spun, so she slowly edged downward, fearing she might faint and pitch to the ground headfirst. Her own blood ran along an arm and down her back, burning like it was on fire. Finally, she found herself huddled up against the base of the statue. The stone steps were cool and she rested against them, facing away from the burning demon and the thick stench it created.

A soft breeze touched her face, making her shiver. The siren was closer now, as well as swirling lights. She looked over, past Robbie's remains, to where she'd left Bess, and found the woman staggering out from one of the crypt.

Only one out of four alive. I so blew this.

A car door slammed from somewhere outside the graveyard. Maybe it was Beck and he'd help her figure out who'd done this. Make them pay.

With a groan of pain, Riley looked upward at the stars, thankful for the opportunity to be able to do that one more time. Her sight cleared and the noble face of the statue above her made her smile. The daughter of a history teacher, she'd know this guy anywhere.

The solemn face of President Abraham Lincoln watched the Archfiend's unholy bonfire, but offered no comment.

"Thanks, Abe," she whispered. "I owe you one."

Chapter Four

"Miss?" a man called out. "What happened here? Are ya hurt?"

It took Riley a moment to figure out what the cop had said, his Scottish accent was so thick.

"Ah, yeah, but not bad." At least she hoped that was the case since her back was screaming in agony and her arm as well. Still, she wasn't dead and that counted for a lot when you went up against an Archfiend.

The cop's concerned gaze went searching behind her and then his eyes widened. "What is that burnin'?"

"A demon," she said, her eyes moving to the flames. It was better than looking down at her hands. She couldn't feel them anyway so that meant they were probably charred little stumps now. "It touched holy ground."

Edinburgh's finest needed to know the rest. "There are three people dead," Riley said. "The demon ... tossed two of over the wall and one's still in the graveyard ... in ... pieces." She sucked in another breath. "There's a woman named Bess over there," she said, indicating the general direction. "I don't think she's hurt."

"A demon, ya say?" The young cop muttered something under his breath she didn't catch, most likely the Scottish version of "Why me?"

Standing, he keyed his radio and called for backup to the Old Calton Burial Ground. The verbal response came quickly and he gave her a nod of reassurance "We'll have an ambulance here soon enough."

"Thanks. How'd you find me?" she asked.

"Someone heard screams and called it in. But I never thought..."

he said, his eyes moving back to the roasting Hellspawn.

"One never does."

When other cops arrived, the first one set off to help Bess. Riley's wounds were starting to kick in now, letting her know that the toxins were moving through her system; a parting gift from the Archfiend, the opportunity to rot from the inside out if the wounds weren't treated soon.

"Riley?" a panicked voice cried out.

It belonged to the one man she'd been praying would find her.

Denver Beck ran full tilt up the steps that led from the street, and then veered toward her, skidding to a halt in front of Lincoln's monument, his backpack hanging loosely off a shoulder. He was in a heavy leather jacket and jeans, his face flushed, his blond hair disheveled. He stared down at her, as if not trusting his eyes, then fell to his knees. A shaking hand reached toward her as if he was trying to ensure she wasn't a mirage.

"Oh, thank God, yer alive," he said as his fingers gently touched her face, demon blood at all.

"Hey, Backwoods Boy," Riley said, trying to lighten the moment with his special nickname. "Sorry things didn't work out ... like we planned."

"Yer hurt," he said simply.

"Just need some Holy Water." She coughed deeply, the smoke from the fiend getting in her lungs.

"What the hell happened here?"

"Some necromancer just had to summon a demon."

Beck checked out the flames over her shoulder. "What kind was it?"

"Archfiend."

He whistled under his breath. "Damn girl, yer awesome," his voice resonating with pride. Beck carefully took hold of her and pulled her close. He smelled of aftershave and fear.

No matter what he said, Riley didn't feel awesome. It could have easily gone the other way and then she would never have seen Beck again. Never felt him gently brush aside her tangled hair or carefully wipe the blood off her face with his rough finger.

Beck pulled back, a false smile in place. "And here I was worried about ya."

Her heart did some little fluttery thing, and for a moment the pain diminished. But she knew he was faking it – Beck's speech was heavy with "ya's" instead of "you's", a verbal barometer of his high stress level.

Then his smile vanished and he glared around. "Where are the bastards that took ya? Are they here?"

"Mostly dead," she said. "The demon got them."

"Good," he replied without hesitation. "Damned good, or they would have been dead when I got done with them." His anger deflated. "Yer safe now, Riley. I promise. I won't let anyone hurt ya."

She really wanted to believe that.

"Miss Blackthorne?" She looked up into the grim face of a man in his early sixties. He wore a brown coat, black slacks and had silver at his temples, his hair pulled back in a ponytail.

"Riley, this is Grand Master MacTavish," Beck said, rising now.

From what Beck had told her, MacTavish was teaching him battle tactics and religious history. He was also one of the most respected members of the International Demon Trappers Guild. A big dog in a kennel full of them.

No matter his rank, Riley was too tired and scared to keep her mouth on a leash. "Hi," she said wearily. "Nice to meet you, sir. Do you throw this kind of welcome for everyone who comes to Scotland, or am I just special?"

The faint hint of a smile curved up the corners of his mouth. "Yer just special, lass." He studied the flames. "Archfiends do make a merry blaze, don't they? How'd ya get it ta touch holy ground?"

How did you know it was an Archfiend?

She didn't ask the question, but gave a quick report on the battle. That earned her a nod of respect.

"That's the second one ya've killed." MacTavish's face stretched into a full smile. "Stewart told me ya were a formidable trapper, and by God, he's right."

Riley shrugged, though it made her shoulder hurt. "Sometimes

I get lucky." She started coughing again, and Beck handed over a bottle of water he'd dug out of his backpack. It promptly dropped out of her hands. Looking down, she was relieved to see all of her fingers were still there, and though they were numb, they appeared completely normal.

Beck took the hint and held the bottle for her. After a long drink, and at MacTavish's urging, she told them what had gone down – how she'd been suckered away from the airport and how everyone but Robbie thought they were summoning an angel.

"I knew they weren't," she said. "It felt wrong. Robbie knew exactly what he was doing. The others were just trying to help Bess' daughter."

MacTavish was frowning now. "The summoner's society has a lot ta answer for."

A police officer led Bess down the path. When she saw Riley she stumbled to a halt. "I'm sorry," she said, her voice quavering with emotion. "I didn't know he was going to do that."

"Who gave Robbie the spell?" Riley asked.

"I don't know. He wouldn't tell us. He just said it'd help Mavis and I believed him. Now my daughter is going to ... die and..."

She lowered her head, weeping inconsolably, as the cop lead her out of the graveyard.

"We need to treat yer wounds," Beck said. "We shouldn't put that off much longer."

While he rummaged in his backpack for the Holy water, Riley closed her eyes, ignoring the bustle around her.

She'd killed an Archfiend, fought Hell one more time and won. She felt no joy in that. Three people were dead, and whoever had put Robbie up to this disaster wasn't one of them.

~ – ~ ~

The police station was noisy and crowded. Apparently it didn't matter what country you were in, everybody had problems, some nastier than others. A few people stared at Riley as she was escorted to an interview room. She could imagine what they thought had happened to her, and almost all of those guesses would be wrong. The cops stared as well – they would know the truth – and some pointedly moved out of her way.

That's me, the Riley of Mass Destruction.

At least she hadn't totally trashed the graveyard, not like last spring in Atlanta. That battle had required a few of Heaven's angels to put Oakland Cemetery back together.

Maybe someday she'd go back to *this* graveyard, see what it looked like in the sunlight. It was probably pretty, or had been before a demon had paid it a visit.

The interview room was chilly and that didn't help. She huddled in a rough blanket, shivering, knowing that some of that was from the wounds. Though Beck had treated those, and a paramedic had bandaged her, he admitted the Holy Water he'd used was a few days old. To be most effective, it should be recently blessed by a priest.

Beck must have guessed what she was thinking. "Brennan is fetchin' some fresh Holy Water. I'll treat yer wounds again once we're at the hotel."

"Okay." Another shiver overtook her, but she tried to ignore it. "Are you still sick?" she asked.

"I'm good. Just some stomach flu thing. Not a big deal."

It had been big enough to keep him from picking her up at the airport. Now, as she studied Beck closer, she could see the dark circles under his eyes and his sallow skin.

"You sure?"

He nodded. "I'm good now that I know yer safe."

Riley forcibly pushed her worries aside: they'd both be feeling better soon, and then they'd start over, make this a real vacation.

No one is going to ruin my time with him.

A woman police constable delivered a large cup of strong tea, laced with sugar. A scone was offered, and since Riley hadn't had anything to eat since the plane, she wolfed it down. A second and a third followed in short order and she made them disappear as well.

Beck took hold of her hand and squeezed it. "That's better," he said, nodding. "If yer eatin', yer gonna be all right."

Riley smiled wanly just because it would make him happy.

The door swung open and two cops entered, both in suits, both with stern expressions. Three dead bodies would do that. Riley knew how this went: they were the detectives and they would have all the questions. Hopefully she would have the right answers.

Two hours later it was all over. The cops had asked all their questions and Riley had tried to answer them as accurately as possible. Now, as she rose from the chair in the interview room, her balance faltered and Beck had to steady her.

"Let's get you to the hotel," he said. "A good night's sleep will help a lot."

Riley forced herself to concentrate on taking one step at a time as they were led out the station house's rear entrance. A young man with light brown hair waited for them near a sleek black car. He looked to be a bit older than Beck.

"Riley, this is David Brennan," Beck said, gesturing. "The real one."

The man looked chagrined at the comment. "Pleased to meet you, Ms. Blackthorne," he said, his accent American. "I'm sorry for what happened."

Makes two of us.

"Brennan's a demon trapper from Los Angeles," Beck explained. "He's been working at the manor for the last six months or so."

"I'm hoping that someday I'll be a grand master," Brennan added.

That comment jarred her. "Why would you want to face that kind of hell?" Riley asked, bewildered.

"Why not?" he said.

Maybe Brennan didn't realize that the death of a Fallen angel was required for entrance into that small, but lethal group. Or that the majority of people who encountered one of Lucifer's angels died on the spot, or surrendered their souls to Hell. Maybe he thought he'd be one of the fortunate ones, though the odds were against him. *Against all of them.*

For a second, Riley didn't want to get in the car with him. What if this was just another trap and Beck didn't realize it?

"It's okay. You'll be fine," Beck said quietly.

More than his reassuring tone, his use of "you" instead of "ya" told her he'd finally calmed down. Told her he trusted Brennan, which meant she could as well.

When the car pulled onto the street, Riley was surprised to see that there were only a few reporters queued up in front of the police station, not like the horde there would have been in Atlanta.

"Where's all the news guys?" she asked.

Brennan's eyes met hers in the rearview mirror. "Grand Master MacTavish made sure there was a news blackout, at least for the time being. The few that are here are just sniffing around, hoping to get thrown a bone or two."

"He won't be able to keep it quiet for long. Not with three bodies," Riley said.

"MacTavish knows that. There's a lot of questions that need answers," Beck said solemnly.

Yeah. Like who had me kidnapped and how they knew I was coming to see you.

~ - ~ - ~

To Riley's relief she'd been ushered into the hotel via a rear entrance, not through the main lobby where everyone could stare at the girl with the bloodied and torn clothes. That had been Beck's doing, and at his insistence Brennan had made the proper arrangements.

"Thank you," she whispered. Beck gave her a faint smile in return. She could see the guilt on his face – he was blaming himself for this disaster, and it would be hard to convince him otherwise.

"I'll take it from here," Beck said once the room key was in his possession. He accepted a plastic bag Brennan offered him.

"There's bandages and tape in there, as well as freshly-consecrated Holy water." Brennan frowned, then continued. "Call if you need anything. I'm staying in town overnight."

Then he was gone, as if he couldn't wait to get away from them.

It was only when Riley reached their room that she realized

something was missing. "Ah crap," she said sinking onto the bed. "My backpack and suitcase are in Robbie's car."

No cell phone, no passport or clothes. No shampoo, makeup, or any of the special small presents she'd brought over for her guy. Not even the new dress she'd bought just for him.

The tears she'd held back began to gang up on her.

Beck quietly stripped off his coat and then dialed the number from the business card the police inspector had given him. He explained the situation, got his answer, and then ended the call.

"The cops are checkin' them for fingerprints. They'll have someone bring them over when they're done."

"Oh, good," she said, sniffling. But that meant some forensics dude was going to be seeing her new underwear, the royal blue lacy ones she'd bought just for this trip. Just for Beck.

Great.

"You need a shower," Beck said. "Then I'll treat yer wounds again."

He was taking charge, just like he had that night when she'd returned from her journey to Hell, shell shocked and so very frightened.

Afraid she'd totally lose it now that the danger was over, which would just upset him further, Riley refused Beck's help and took refuge in the bathroom, closing the door after her. Even when it proved difficult to get her jeans unzipped and her bra off with her numb fingers, she refused to ask for assistance. It was even harder to strip off the bandages and get the shower set properly, but eventually she was under the water, feeling it sting and burn in so many places besides her arm and shoulder. The blood made the water pink and she had to swallow repeatedly not to vomit.

Why couldn't it have been like I planned? Why does everything go wrong?

By the time she had climbed out of the shower there was a pair of Beck's sweatpants and a roomy tee shirt lying on the counter, though she hadn't heard him bring them in. Riley pulled on the pants, tightening the drawstring so they wouldn't end up around her knees. After dousing her wounds in the fresh Holy Water, she clamped her eyes shut as pain rippled through her body. Trying to visualize the cuts healing didn't work, instead her mind went muzzy, her heart beat picking up speed and she found it hard to breathe. She clung onto the sink until the dizziness and nausea passed. Treating demon wounds was ugly, but not usually this bad.

When Riley finally looked in the mirror, she winced. The dark circles under her eyes stood out against pale skin and there was a big bruise on her left collarbone. A single tear tracked down her cheek now, dropping into the sink, a wet testimony to how much this sucked.

She'd dreamed of this day for months, how she'd step off the plane and Den would be there to hold her, kiss her, tell her how much he loved her. She'd saved up extra money to have her hair trimmed and even added special highlights. Then there was the manicure and pedicure, and a few special new clothes. All with one goal in mind: spending time with the man she loved.

Now she was sliced and bruised and sick, all because some idiot had wanted to meet a demon in person.

A tentative tap came at the door. "Riley? You okay?"

No. It's never going to be okay again.

"Riley?"

She couldn't hide in the bathroom forever – her wounds needed bandaging – so she didn't bother to put on the tee shirt, just clutched it close to cover her chest. When she opened re-entered the bedroom Beck's worried eyes watching her intently.

"I have some hot chocolate for you," he said.

Usually her heart would have melted at his thoughtfulness, but not this time. She really wanted to tell him to leave her alone.

Instead, she bit her tongue as he played nursemaid.

"These wounds aren't as deep as I thought they'd be," he said with obvious relief. "You were lucky."

Unlike the three people who died.

Riley refused the drink and settled on the bed, letting the tee shirt fall away. There was no amount of hot chocolate in this world to fix this mess.

Beck laid out the bandages, one by one. "We make a good team, you and me. One of us gets hurt, the other is there to help," he said.

She didn't reply.

"You want to talk about what happened now, or in the mornin'?"

"Morning," she mumbled, buying time. Or maybe never. He'd heard what she'd told the cops and MacTavish. Wasn't that enough? Why was he pushing her like this? Why couldn't he just back off?

She ground her teeth instead of talking as Beck applied fresh bandages. He carefully placed one on the knife wound and then helped her pull on the tee shirt.

"That's better," he said.

No, it's not.

Afraid she'd say something hurtful, Riley climbed in the bed. She pushed aside the down comforter. She wouldn't need it, not with Beck lying next to her. The guy was a constant furnace, summer or winter.

She laid on her right side, facing the wall, her left arm throbbing with each heartbeat. When Beck slid in next to her a light kiss fell on her cheek.

"I love you," he said. "I missed you so much."

It was what she wanted to hear, but deep in her heart there was still that weird unease, a sense of foreboding.

No matter what Beck thought, this wasn't over. Whoever had tried to make her a demon sacrifice wasn't going to back off.

Maybe the next time she wouldn't be so lucky.

Chapter Five

When Riley woke, the clock on the nightstand indicated it was ten-thirty. She rolled over and fought down a groan. Her arm was aching, as was most her body; she had to be one massive bruise. Riley kicked off the covers, too warm from the toxins the demon wounds had set loose. At least this time she wasn't as sick as when she'd tangled with a Grade Three demon and nearly died.

To get her mind off her pains, Riley checked out the room. The space was bigger than she'd expected, with a desk, a wardrobe, a couch and a couple of chairs.

I'm in Scotland. How cool is that?

Not as cool as she'd planned after the previous night's disaster.

Stop being a grump.

Beck was on the couch, sitting in a pool of light cast by a reading lamp, his head bent over a book. Once his reading skills had improved, he was making up for lost time. He still read slowly, but now he wasn't mouthing words or using his finger to follow along.

Her boyfriend was dressed in a long sleeved navy blue tee shirt and jeans, and though that wasn't unusual, there was something different in the way he held himself. He seemed older, more confident, as if he'd come to terms with who he was and what role he had to play in this world.

Riley had begun to feel the same way, at least until this trip. To suddenly to find herself a pawn of people she didn't even know had shaken her to the core.

Was this their future, a lifetime of looking over their shoulders, wondering when the next lunatic would try to kill her or steal her blood to conjure up a demon?

The answer was a resounding "Yes."

The tiniest whimper fled Riley's lips before she could stop it and the sound caught Beck's attention.

He looked over at her and then smiled, clearly pleased she was awake.

"Hey, sleepyhead," he said, his tone light, as if she'd just awoken in his house back in Atlanta.

Beck was going for the "let's move on with our lives" tone. Two could play that game.

"Hey, you. What's the book about?"

"Four hundred and..." he thumbed to the back, "forty-nine pages of how Hell goes about acquirin' souls. They've got some mean-assed tricks up their sleeves. Like we don't know that already." He closed the book and dropped it inside his duffle bag. Then he joined her, sitting on the side of the bed. His hair was longer, touching his collar now. That was unheard of for Beck, but it made him even more handsome in her eyes, if that was possible.

"How are you feelin'?" he asked.

"Sore." She began to scratch at the bandage on the left arm, which led him to carefully remove it. One of the claw marks was completely closed, an angry red line against her tanned skin. The other two were better, still healing.

"Best I treat those wounds again. I didn't want to wake you. You were so tired."

"Just jet lag," she said.

They both knew it was more than that.

After she'd used the toilet he joined her in the bathroom where he gave the arm wounds another dose of Holy Water. He did the same with the shoulder wound, and then the knife slice, out of habit, though it would have no effect.

Once again the nausea and the muzziness hit Riley hard, and he helped steady her.

"You should go back to bed," he said.

Riley shook her head.

"Okay, but we need to get you some food. You wanna eat in the room, or go out?" he asked as he capped the Holy Water and set it on the counter.

It was a simple question, but one that had no easy answer. If she refused to leave the hotel then those idiot necros would destroy her vacation. Still, to go out into the real world meant she'd have to accept that she was a target. That she would always be one.

"I won't let anythin' happen to you," he said softly, touching her cheek with such gentleness it nearly made her cry.

"I know," she said. "But I don't have anything to wear." At least nothing that wasn't covered in dirt and blood.

"Yer suitcase and backpack were delivered a couple hours ago," he replied. "The lady cop said she was the one who handled your clothes so no guys saw yer girlie stuff."

Score! That brightened her up immensely.

Once she was bandaged, Riley retrieved a fresh pair of undies out of the top zippered section of her suitcase as well as a pair of jeans and shirt, then retreated to the bathroom again.

As the door closed behind her, Beck sighed. He knew her in all her moods: happy, grieving, angry, and defiant. He'd seen her hit the wall so hard he was sure she'd shatter. She'd been that way after her father had died and the time she'd been carried off to Hell by the Fallen angel. Every time Riley had risen stronger and more resilient.

Usually she would say something to let him know where her head was, but not this time. She was too withdrawn, and that troubled him. Some of it was shock and that was understandable; you did not step off an airplane expecting to walk into your boyfriend's arms and instead become demon bait without experiencing a lot of conflicting emotions. Still, Beck felt it was more than that. Was she mad at him for not being there for her? Did she think he didn't care?

He ran a hand through his hair, his worry escalating. Something was wrong between them, he could feel it, and he wasn't sure what it was.

The door opened and Riley walked to the couch, though at

half speed. His question as to what she wanted to do was answered when she put on her shoes and then a heavy sweater. Despite the horrors she'd experienced, Riley was willing to go out onto the streets, put herself in danger again.

This time you won't be on yer own.

This time he would protect her with his life.

~ ~ ~ ~ ~

Beck had roamed around Edinburgh every other weekend, unless he'd been buried in *research,* as MacTavish called it. Beck didn't complain; he was learning more about the war between Heaven and Hell, who had been on which side, and how many people had found their lives ripped to pieces by the eternal conflict. He'd found himself increasingly concerned that he and Riley's relationship might suffer the same fate.

They were walking along High Street now, letting her gain a sense of the town. "Cool, isn't it?" he said, pulling himself back to the present.

Riley nodded, her eyes taking in the scenery. "The buildings are so ... old. Not like Atlanta."

He'd thought the same each time he'd come to Edinburgh. Usually it was on Saturdays or Sundays, a chance to get away from the manor house and his small room. Sometimes he'd bunk in a hostel overnight, sometimes he'd make the round trip the same day.

But it was more than getting out of his room – he was living in a country so full of history it almost bubbled out of the ground. Deep in his heart he knew that Paul would have been proud of him taking this risk, seizing this chance to better himself.

"How are you doin'?" Beck asked, noticing that Riley was quiet again.

"Okay."

No, you're not.

He caught her uninjured arm and steered her down one of the small closes, an alley that cut off the Royal Mile.

"If yer not good with bein' out we can–" he began.

"No!" she said, cutting him off. "I want to see stuff. I didn't fly all the way over here to hide in some hotel room."

Despite the defiance, he heard the naked fear as well.

"Okay. So what do you want to see first – the castle, the gardens or a museum?"

She blinked at him in surprise. "You go to museums now?"

"Sure," he said, trying not to be offended. "There's lots of cool stuff to see. Just tell me what you want to do."

The frown formed instantly. "What I wanted was something perfect. That's why I had my hair fixed and got a manicure and bought new jeans and..." Her lower lip began to quiver.

Then some bastards ruined it for you.

"But people died, Den," she said, her voice quieter now. "So me whining about all that is ... silly."

"No, it's righteous. You were hurt. You were really lookin' forward to seein' me."

Riley nodded and walked into his arms. "I missed you so much."

They hugged for a time as people flowed by them on the nearby street.

"I like what you did with your hair," he said, touching one of the lighter strands. "It's really pretty."

When Riley beamed up at him, he knew it'd been the right thing to say. Not that she needed to do anything to her hair – she was beautiful to him no matter what.

"Thanks. Simi talked me into the highlights. I was hoping you'd like them."

"As long as they're not one of those weird colors she wears, I'm good."

When Riley leaned back, her hands on his chest, he could see her chipped fingernail polish. Maybe that was the best place to start.

"I can't change a thing about what happened to you, but we can begin over, Riley. We can make sure they don't screw up the time we have left."

He saw a tiny spark of life flash in her eyes. "We can?"

"Yup. So let's act like I just picked you up at the airport and I brought you to town. Can you do that?"

She thought about it, then nodded.

"Good," He grabbed onto her before she could protest, being careful not to hurt her. The kiss went on for some time. When it ended they were both out of breath.

"Welcome to Scotland, Riley."

A shy smile came his way. "I love you, Den."

"Right back at you," he said, taking her hand.

He strolled her along the Royal Mile and then turned north, toward New Town. When they found themselves in a street market, Riley began to loosen up, slowly shaking off the last twenty-four hours.

As they shopped, Riley bought a book on Scottish history and tucked it into his backpack. He talked her into a pair of pretty earrings at an estate sale booth and she seemed very pleased he'd bought them for her.

Then her jaw dropped.

"What is it?"

"Look!" she said, pointing at a jewelry case. It took him a bit to notice exactly which item she was pointing at, but when he did he blinked in surprise. A quick look at his grandmother's ring on her right hand confirmed his first impression. His gran's ring was a solid silver band with ivy engraved into the metal. This one had the same design, but also a single small red gem nestled flush in the band. A ruby, perhaps?

"Wow, can you believe it?" she said. "They've both got that ivy pattern."

"It's really pretty. You want to try it on?" he asked.

"What? No. It's really nice, but I have this one," she said, raising her hand. "I don't need another."

"You sure?"

"Yeah. Besides, it'd be too much money."

As she walked on, Beck leaned over asked the vendor how much the ring cost. He was pleased to learn it wasn't as bad as he'd figured.

When he caught up with Riley, she was digging through a stack of old books, but he caught her looking over her shoulder at the ring one last time.

~ ~ ~ ~ ~

As the day progressed, Riley kept feeling that someone was following them. Even Beck noticed her skittishness.

"No one's taggin' along after us. I can tell."

She wasn't sure if he was fibbing or not. What if whoever was following them was one of *his* people, someone who answered to the grand masters? Who else would have known her schedule? Maybe they were going to make another run at her...

Quit, will you? It wasn't like her to be so paranoid. Cautious, yes. Totally crazy? *No way.*

As they wandered down a long street filled with shops, all kinds of merchandise beckoned to her, but when she tried to calculate how much something would cost in American money, her brain seized up. That wasn't normal – she could always do math in her head.

Jetlag strikes again.

Beck paused in front of a nail salon, then pulled out some Scottish bills and handed it over. "Get those nails fixed up, okay? Take yer time. We're in no hurry. We're on vacation, right?"

In his own way he was helping her get on with her life.

"I won't take too long," she promised, touched by his kindness.

"Just text me when yer done." She hesitated. "You'll be safe here. Don't worry."

With a rushed kiss on his cheek Riley entered the shop, wondering if they had the same colors of nail polish as they did back home.

It took about thirty minutes before she was back on the street, looking for Beck. She'd texted him that she was done and he'd said he be waiting for her. When he wasn't, the fear began to rise again. What if something had happened to him? Or what if he had left her alone on purpose?

Then she saw him hurrying toward her and when he spied her,

he broke out in a wide smile.

Where were you? What were you doing?

Riley shook aside those thoughts as Beck admired her nails. He said he loved the color – something called Coldstream Blue – and then suggested they head toward Princes Street Gardens. There, in the late afternoon sun, they picnicked with hot meat pies and an orange and almost bubble gum flavored drink called Irn Bru. For Riley there was even a piece of fudge.

"You eat like this every time you come to Edinburgh?" she asked, licking the chocolate off her fingers.

"No, usually I pack my lunch. Sometimes I climb to the top of Arthur's Seat and stay until dark. Watch the lights come on."

"Like you do at home, then."

"Yeah, except it's even prettier here."

Suddenly she wanted to be up there with him, and when she mentioned it, he shook his head. "Tomorrow night."

"Why not tonight?"

"We're both tired and you're sore from ... the flight."

He was trying too hard now and she called him on it.

"Just want you happy," he said, looking away.

Her suspicions rose again. "Someone knew I was going to be at the airport. Who did you tell?"

When he raised his eyes she saw worry. "Only the people at the manor house. No one else."

She'd told a few people in Atlanta, but those were friends. No one who would want to hurt her. Whoever had set her kidnapping in motion was close to the grand masters. *Close to Beck.*

"I'm tired. I need to go back to the hotel," Riley said, rising abruptly.

"You okay?" he asked, worried.

"Fine."

I just need time to figure out who I can trust.

Chapter Six

After Riley had taken a long nap, they'd wandered around for another couple of hours as Beck showed her hidden spots in the city – leave it to him to do a complete reconnaissance of a town. She'd been surprised the first time he'd paused to drop a few coins in the paper cup of a homeless person.

When he rejoined her, he murmured, "I got a lot to thankful for. Those guys remind me of that every day." After that, she knew to slow down as he stopped by each of them, wishing them well and leaving behind a bit of money.

When Riley's hunger had flared up Beck took her to the Mitre Bar on the Royal Mile, bought her a sandwich and some tomato soup. He'd settled for fish and chips and a beer. Then, to her surprise, he'd ordered a whisky.

"Do you like it over here?" she asked in between spoonfuls of soup.

"I really do," he said. "It's not home, but the folks are friendly and the place is so damned beautiful. Edinburgh's nice, but wait 'til you see the Highlands. It's like God's own country."

"You sound like Stewart now," she joked.

"I see why he wants to move back here. I would if I was Scottish. Sure, some of the folks are kinda screwed up, but no more so than in Atlanta. I could live here, you know?"

That was a surprise. He'd always been a total Georgia boy.

It was like watching a moth spin a cocoon and then magically change into a butterfly. It was clear that by the time Beck returned to Atlanta, he'd be someone different.

What if that someone doesn't want me anymore?

She studied him anew. What else hadn't he told her about his training? How far would he go to become a grand master? Would he give her up just to make the cut?

Riley shook herself. Why would she ever think that Beck would leave her behind?

Because he could do just that.

After Beck shut the door to the hotel room behind them, the chain and deadbolt went in place. Then he tested each of them; apparently Riley wasn't the only one who was spooked.

He took his shower first, mostly because she wanted to send an e-mail to Peter. He'd already written her twice and was getting edgy because she hadn't replied. Once she was done telling him some of the gruesome details, she surfed for a while. There appeared to be nothing new happening in Atlanta and nothing in the way of news about a demon summoning in Edinburgh. She found Beck watching over her shoulder.

"Anythin'?" he asked.

"They claim some kids were caught vandalizing Old Calton Burial Ground," she said. "They don't mention the dead people at all."

"MacTavish asked the cops to hold back for a bit, at least until he can figure out who did this."

"The International Guild has that much power?"

"Yeah. Almost as much as the Vatican."

Whoa. That meant they could do whatever they wanted to news stories ... or to people who got in their way. *Like me?*

She'd never really given it much thought, but now she wondered if the grand masters were happy about her and Beck being together. He'd never said anything, but he might not if he thought it would upset her.

A knock came at the door, startling her. Beck crossed quickly to the portal, checked through the peephole, then undid the locks. Brennan beckoned him outside and Beck complied, closing the door behind him. Tempting as it was to eavesdrop, Riley stayed put. The conversation was quiet, and though she didn't hear the specifics, she suspected they weren't discussing their favorite pubs or the best place to buy haggis.

Beck returned, securing the locks once again.

"What was that about?"

"Nothin'," he said. He was cutting her out of the loop, again.

You weren't like this at home. "Is this the way it's going to be from now on? You keeping secrets from me?"

Beck sat on the end of the bed, looking more tired than she had seen him in a long time. "There will be things I can't tell you, Riley. It has to be that way."

"Or what? If you do they'll kill me or something?"

His eyes widened, but he made no reply. His stunned expression made her regret suggesting such a thing.

Riley took a deep breath, trying to settle down. "Sorry. So ... what *can* you tell me?"

His nod said he accepted her apology. "Brennan was lettin' me know that the woman they arrested, the one named Bess ... her daughter is gettin' worse."

All because they couldn't summon an angel.

"Those guys were set up, Beck. None of them had that much power and they shouldn't have been anywhere near that kind of spell. That's way above their skill set."

Before he could reply, his phone pinged and he checked the message. Then promptly blanked it as if it was a state secret.

She'd had enough. "I don't like that you can't tell me everything, like I can't be trusted."

Beck put on his stone face. "I'm not likin' it anymore than you are," he replied. "But it comes with the territory."

Maybe not. When they'd started dating there hadn't been any of this "I can't tell you" nonsense. There was just demon trapping, not some secret organization of grand masters who had their fingers in all sorts of pies.

Now it's all about you and them. What happened to us?

Beck sat in bed, trying to read, but it was useless. Riley's emotions were all over the map now – fine one minute, in his face the next.

Give her some time.

Still, she did have a point; there was stuff he couldn't tell her, secret knowledge that had been passed down from century to century. He'd found it so amazing when he'd first started down this path, but now he saw how his job could hurt a relationship. MacTavish had warned him about that, but Beck had reassured him that Riley would be okay with it all.

Now he wasn't so sure.

She exited the bathroom holding one of his tee shirts.

"Did you treat the wounds?" he asked.

"Yeah. They still hurt."

After he reapplied the bandages, Beck turned off the light on the nightstand as she settled in next to him. If this had been at home, they'd forget the bad stuff, lose themselves in each other's loving. But Riley didn't turn to him now.

He ran his fingertips down her uninjured arm, savoring the scent of her.

"Night, Den," she whispered, and then closed her eyes.

He sighed. It wasn't going to be easy to sleep next to her and not want more, but he wouldn't push it. In some ways, it felt as if they were starting all over again.

It'll be better tomorrow.

Beck put his arm around her and she snuggled closer, laying her head on his chest.

"Sorry, I can't tell you everythin'" he said. "But I can tell you some things."

Riley shifted her head so she could see his face. "Like what??"

"You never asked what happened to me when I was in Hell," he said.

"I wasn't sure if you wanted to talk about it."

"Well, it's time you know."

Riley listened in silence as he told her what had happened after he'd been wounded by Sartael's blade. What he'd endured while she'd sat vigil over him. How he'd known he was dying, how much it hurt to realize that he'd never see her again.

"You've been to Hell, you know what it's like," he said.

"For me, maybe, but not for you. Ori said it was different for everyone, even a Fallen."

Beck grew pensive at the mention of her first lover. "Lucifer said if I gave him my soul I'd live, I'd come back to you and no one would ever know what I'd done."

Riley jerked in surprise. "God, you didn't. You couldn't..."

"No, I didn't," he admitted. "I love you more than anythin' in this world, but I could not give up my soul. If I was dead, it was all I had left I could call my own."

Riley bowed her head in relief. "Then how did you get out of Hell?"

"My momma. Sadie showed me the way out. Can you believe it?" he said, his voice catching at the end. "I thought she hated me."

"No, I think she loved you in her own weird way."

Perhaps now it was time to ask a question of his own. "Down at the hospital that day, when she was dyin'. What did she say to you?"

Riley looked up at him. "I'm surprised you haven't asked me that before now."

"Wasn't sure if I'd like the answer."

She nodded her understanding. "Your mother made me promise to keep you safe."

It was his turn to bow his head. "I never understood that woman."

"I don't think she understood herself."

As she fell asleep, Riley cuddled close to him. No matter how tired he was, Beck remained awake.

Somethin's changed. He wasn't sure if it was between them, or something bigger on the horizon. One thing he did know; until he knew for sure, he'd keep his worries to himself.

~ ~ ~ ~

When Riley woke, the room was in twilight, the heavy curtains pulled closed once again. For a moment she thought she'd slept the entire day. A glance at the clock proved it was closer to nine in the morning.

She'd woken up once overnight, and out of habit had treated her deepest wounds and bandaged them. Beck had slumbered on, without knowing she'd gotten out of bed.

Now she heard a faint voice through the door to the bathroom; he was talking to Stewart about her.

Reporting back to your masters?

"Don't worry," Beck said, his voice louder now. "I'll keep her safe. I give you my word on that."

And just like that the distrust faded. If Beck gave his word, it was solid gold.

He does love me. And I love him.

So why did she feel so unsure about him now?

Riley flopped back on the bed and stared at the ceiling, confused. Other than a few kisses he'd not tried to rekindle what they'd shared in Atlanta. It was like he didn't care for her anymore, at least not in *that* way.

She thumped her forehead with the palm of her hand.

Stop it!

The bathroom door opened and Beck paused when he saw she was awake. Instead of looking guilty, he seemed pleased. "Did I wake you?"

She shook her head.

"I was talking to Stewart, letting him know how you were doing. He sends his love."

"Is he freaking out?"

"A little. His cough is better."

"That's good news."

With a big smile, Beck sat on the side of the bed. "Happy Birthday!" he said. "How's it feel to be eighteen?"

Birthday? Riley had totally forgotten it, which was major weird. *Wow, the jet lag is seriously kicking my butt.*

"It *is* my birthday. So why I don't feel any different?"

"I never do. It's just a number thing." He kissed her forehead and she inhaled the scent of soap and aftershave.

"So Princess, you wanna go see a castle?"

Part of her did and other part just wanted to lay here and stare at the ceiling. *What is up with that?* She was in Scotland with her guy. She could chill at home.

"Sure," Riley said, trying to sound excited. "Let me do the Holy Water thing and get dressed."

~ ~ ~ ~ ~

In his own way, Beck made sure her birthday was as special as he could make it. They had lunch at the castle, visited more bookshops, then as the afternoon wore away he suggested they make a trip to Arthur's Seat right before sunset. He insisted it was a grand view of Edinburgh eight hundred and some feet above the city.

Riley studied the massive rock. "We're climbing that?"

Beck laughed. "No. I wouldn't do that to you. I want you in good shape once we get to the top."

She heard something in his voice that told this was more than a mere hiking expedition.

A few minutes later, Beck flagged down a cab and the driver took them as far up the hill as was possible. After he'd arranged for the guy to return in an hour, they began the ascent. Riley kept her eyes on the path, and soon was rewarded with labored breathing and a dripping nose.

Will he ask me to marry him up here?

That would be just like him. Though she tried, Riley couldn't get a handle on her feelings. She loved him. He loved her. Why was she so uneasy?

I'm just nervous.

Once they reached the top she knew it'd been worth all the effort. Edinburgh lay below them like a complex quilt: Old Town, New Town, the Balmoral Hotel, Sir Walter Scott's memorial, and the castle. In the distance the estuary, the Firth of Forth, sparkled in the waning light.

"This is amazing, Den," she said, searching and then failing to find the Old Calton graveyard where it was hidden among the maze of buildings.

"I love it," he said as he settled on a broad rock that offered a commanding view of the city below. When she shivered in the brisk wind, Beck pulled her closer. "It's even better now that yer here."

That made her smile. "Any Scots in your family?"

"Some, at least on my momma's side. My gran was a Macpherson. Beck is German, so I'm a mutt."

"My family was all English," Riley replied.

She laid her head on his shoulder, content for the moment, though in some ways this peace felt fragile, like hand-blown glass.

In the distance, the sun gradually vanished behind a sea of clouds, creating a deep purple glow. Below, lights began to come on one by one.

"Isn't it beautiful?" he whispered.

"Yes, it is." The passage of time marked by sun and stars.

"I wouldn't want to share this with anyone else," he said, turning toward her. A soft kiss brushed her cheek. She shivered and he tucked her coat collar closer around her neck.

Beck rose and stood a few paces away, his back to her. For a time he stared out at the city, as if composing his thoughts. Then he turned back toward her. With a shy smile, he was down on one knee in heartbeat.

Ohmigod. He's going to do it.

Beck took her hands, stripped off the gloves and then kissed each of her palms. She could feel the brush of his stubble and his warm breath on her fingers.

"Den…"

Denver Beck took a deep breath, preparing himself for what had to be one of the most important times of his life.

"I am a plain Georgia boy," he began, his voice rough. "I always will be. I have many things I love, but none as much as you." He took another quick breath, fearing his courage would falter. "I can't live without you, Riley. Yer in my heart, and in my soul."

God, this is hard. No matter how many times he'd practiced it in front of a mirror.

"I want you to be mine, forever. My wife, the mother of my children. I swear there won't be anyone else but you for as long as I live." He swallowed, trying to clear his suddenly dry throat. He was so nervous now, he could hardly speak. "Will ya ... will you marry me, Riley? Will you stand by me for the rest of my days?"

For godsakes say you will.

His heart hammered and he felt himself sweat as those gorgeous brown eyes widened. He loved her so much, but Riley was just eighteen, and she'd be shackling herself to him for life. Because it *was* all or nothing for him.

There were tears in her eyes now, but still no answer.

"Riley?" he said, his nerves jumping all over the place.

She pulled her hands away and wrapped her arms around herself, withdrawing. "I..." she began.

He saw something in her eyes now, and it wasn't joy. It was more the look of a trapped animal.

She was going to turn him down.

"Riley?" he repeated, his fear growing.

"I can't. I'm not sure why," she said, her voice quavering. "If you'd asked me a week ago, I would have said yes. But now ... I–"

"Are ya mad at me cuz I wasn't there for ya?"

"Yes ... No. God, I don't know," she stammered. "I think ... " Then she shook her head as if she couldn't find the words. "I don't understand what's wrong now, but something is."

Hell! She turned me down. She let me make a fool of myself.

His ego told him it wasn't his fault. In the past, when he'd been some loser, he could have seen her refusing him, but now he was doing good things, making something of himself. He had a future and he'd thought she wanted to share it with him.

What the hell is goin' on in yer head? Have ya just been playin' me all along?

Lurching to his feet, he moved away from her, pointedly putting space between them. When he jammed his hands in his pockets, his fingers touched the box that held the ring – the one she'd seen at the street market. It was why he was being so secretive on the phone the other day, eager to surprise her.

Not now.

He resisted the urge to toss it off the side of the mountain.

She was on her feet now. "Den, I'm—"

He raised his hand for silence. "No need to explain. Ya don't wanna get married to me. I got it. Don't say stuff just to try to make me feel better."

The tears were rolling down her cheeks now. "I'm so sorry."

Not as much as I am.

~ - ~ ~

It had been incredibly somber in the taxi back to the hotel, and even worse in their room. Whatever they'd shared between them was damaged now, perhaps destroyed forever.

Why did I turn him down? She'd been dreaming about this for months, ever since he said he'd wanted her to come to Scotland for her birthday.

What is wrong with me?

Sullen, Beck pulled the extra blankets and a pillow out of the wardrobe and claimed the couch, actions that told her he wouldn't be sharing her bed tonight. Or any night in the future.

Hands shaking, Riley treated her wounds again, letting the Holy Water burn into her flesh. As the liquid cleansed the demon taint, her horror at what she'd done began to fade.

She had a right to say "no" if she wanted. Beck could just deal. It wasn't like he really cared.

But I still love him, don't I?

If so, why did she feel the need to run, to get away from him?

As Riley went through the motions, putting on fresh bandages, tears trickled like a slow leak. She curled up in the bed, alone.

An hour later, unable to sleep, she sat up and looked over at the couch. Beck was still lying there, fully clothed, his hands behind his back as he glowered at the ceiling. When he realized she was watching him, he rose, collected his cell phone, heading for the door.

"Den–"

He halted and did a slow turn, his eyes burning in fury. "Is there some other guy, Riley? Is that what's gonna on here?"

"What? No! How could you even think that?"

"I don't know. How could I possibly think ya'd be wantin' to marry me? Silly old Beck, stupid as ever."

"Den–"

"Just go to sleep," he snarled. "There's nothin' ya can say that'll make it any better."

The door slammed behind him, leaving Riley alone in the dark.

⁓ ⁃ ⁓ ⁃ ⁓

Beck was on his third pint of beer and tempted to just keep drinking. He hadn't felt this empty since the night Paul had died.

Yeah, old friend, yer little girl just kicked me right in the balls.

He sure as hell hadn't seen that coming. Or had he? He sorted back through his memories – Riley all eager and happy, counting down the days before she could see him. Riley upset, but coping right after the demon incident. Even though she'd been injured, she'd been doing okay.

He frowned in thought. *When did she change?*

"Another one, mate?" the hotel bartender asked, gesturing at Beck's empty pint.

"No, thanks," he replied. He had enough of a buzz on as it was. "Got any coffee?"

The man nodded and headed off to fill the order. Beck stared down at the box holding the engagement ring where it sat next to the empty glass of beer. Maybe he could return it and...

Was it just his ego that had taken a hit, or was something else going on?

He checked the time – just a little after eleven. Though he didn't like to share his troubles with anyone, something made him dial Grand Master MacTavish. His superior answered almost immediately.

"How's it goin', lad? Did ya pop the question yet?"

Ah shit.

Beck gave him the grim news and waited for the reaction.

"Ya dinna call me ta say the girl turned ya down. What's really on yer mind?"

"She's different. I know, maybe it's my pride talkin', but my gut says somethin's goin' on with her, and it started when we got to the hotel."

There was a long pause. While Beck waited, a cup of coffee appeared in front of him. He nodded his thanks and took a sip, finding it strong, bitter even, and that helped clear his head.

"How much did she trust ya in the past?" MacTavish asked.

"With her life," Beck said.

"And now she's not trustin' ya at all. Hmmm ... Bring her here tomorrow. I want ta talk ta Riley for a bit, see if she can tell me what's goin' on."

"She hasn't told me," Beck snapped.

"Yer too close ta her. If it's a matter that she's got cold feet, then we'll know that. If it's somethin' else..."

"Like what?"

"We'll see when ya get here."

"Did you find out how many people knew about her comin' to Scotland?" Beck asked.

"Aye. Includin' the two of us, there were eight: Kepler and Brennan, of course. Then there's the housekeeper, the cook, the maid, and our travel agent."

"Someone leaked that information and set Riley up," Beck replied. Someone had deliberately screwed up his future.

"I'm not thinkin' they're not done messin' with her yet. Put the hurt behind ya, lad, and keep focused on the problem. We'll sort it one way or the other."

We damned well better.

Chapter Seven

Riley hastily repacked her suitcase after Beck had grumpily rousted her out of bed at eight. He insisted they leave within the hour.

"Where are we going?" she asked.

"To the manor."

"I thought we were going up there later this week."

"We were. Now we're goin' today."

"Orders from your boss?" she said, glaring at him.

"Yeah. Get movin'."

From that point on, they packed in silence. The room felt too small, maybe even the whole planet. If there was some way Riley could fly home today, she would have done it. She had no doubt Beck would have happily let her go. After using the last of the Holy Water and tossing the bottle in the trash, she zipped her suitcase shut.

I shouldn't have come here. I should have stayed home.

Maybe if she could find a way to ditch Beck, she might be able to think this through. But that wasn't likely to happen.

Beck kept snapping at her until they boarded the train, and his surly behavior made her wonder just how much he hated her now. Once they were seated, he seemed to settle down, and his chilly behavior thawed a bit, as if he'd come to terms with her rejection and decided to move on.

He traded texts with Brennan, then, as the train wound its way west through Stirling and then farther north, he extracted a map from his backpack and helped her trace their journey into the Highlands. He'd been right – the scenery was beyond her imagining.

A couple hours later, they left the train at a small Scottish town where Beck led them to a car at the far end of a car park.

When she asked about how it'd gotten there, he said, "Brennan left it here for us."

Brennan again. "He's kind of your all-purpose slave, isn't he?"

"Yeah, but don't tell him that," Beck replied.

"You know how to drive on the left side?"

He nodded. "It's simple once you work it out in yer head."

Until you get back to Atlanta.

As they climbed in she found another bottle of Holy Water on the seat with a note attached:

For Riley

"Your guy Brennan is way efficient."

"He must like ya," was the curt reply.

Riley stuffed the bottle in her backpack – her wounds were healed enough she didn't need it anymore.

As they made their way along a two lane highway, she tried to relax and enjoy the scenery. She'd seen pictures of Scotland, but they weren't close to the real thing. The Highlands were ruggedly beautiful, almost beyond the ability describe to them in mere words. The mountains were covered in trees and there were deep lakes – lochs as they called them.

She found herself relaxing, not feeling the need to escape any longer.

I am so screwed up. She kept taking quick glances at Beck, replaying the night before over and over in her head. Now she felt sick that she'd turned him down. If she'd agreed to marry him, today would be so different, so good. *But I didn't.* And now, on every birthday for the rest of her life, she'd remember that moment on the mountain.

"What do you think?" Beck asked, looking over at her now.

"What? Oh ... Now I know why Stewart loves this place."

"Wait until you see the loch behind the manor house. It's real pretty at sunset."

"What am I getting into here? Are the other grand masters nice or..." *Will they hate me because of what I did to you?*

"There's only one other grand master who lives here – his name is Kepler – and he's in his seventies. His job is to keep track of the archives."

"How many grand masters are there in the world?"

"Twenty-nine. If I'm lucky, I'll be number thirty."

"So few."

"Not many of us survive first contact with a Fallen. You know what they're like."

Ori. Even now his name brought heartache. Was he enjoying the sunrise each morning as the newest gargoyle on the Blackthorne mausoleum back in Atlanta? Or was he as lost as he'd seemed when she'd first met him?

"Yer missin' the angel, aren't you?"

She nodded. "How could you tell?"

"You always look so sad when you hear his name," he said. Beck reached over to squeeze her hand, then stopped himself as if she wasn't worthy of that gesture now. "Personally, I didn't like the bastard, but he did what was right in the end."

"He thought he could keep me safe."

"It was still wrong."

Beck might not mourn Ori's death, but she would in her own way.

"So if there are only twenty-nine grand masters, how do they get anything done? I mean, they can't be everywhere at once."

"They have people who handle things in different countries. That's what Brennan's trainin' to be – one of the International Guild's representatives. They're thinkin' of sendin' him to Mexico since he's fluent in Spanish."

So that's how it all works. She'd always wondered.

"We're almost there," he said. "About a mile left."

Riley wasn't exactly sure what she expected, but the manor house certainly was impressive. Huge by US standards, though probably small by Scottish measures, it was comprised of solid stone. Large windows dotted all four floors and she didn't even try to count the chimneys.

"How old is this place?" she asked.

"The original house was built in the eighteen hundreds but they kept addin' to it," Beck replied. "I remember the first time I saw it. All I could think is 'What the hell is a poor Georgia boy doin' here?'"

"Learning to be a grand master, that's what," she said, trying to smile. It seemed like she'd almost forgotten how.

"I figured they'd toss my ass out first thing, but MacTavish invited me into some sort of sittin' room and handed me a glass of whisky. Then he asked me about what Atlanta was like. So I told him."

"Sizing you up?"

"Yup, but he was so smooth I didn't realize what he was doin' until I found myself talkin' about the tactics we used at the Oakland Cemetery battle."

That conjured up memories that were hard to handle: scores of demons hacking their way through the trappers and the Vatican's Demon Hunters. The dead and dying. Her father. Lord Ozymandias. Sartael and Ori. Then the final confrontation between the forces of Hell and those from Heaven.

"Sorry," he said, looking over at her. "Maybe I shouldn't have mentioned that."

"I'll have to deal with the nightmares someday."

"I never will," he replied, softer now.

Beck parked around the side of the building near two other cars and then helped her bring in her luggage. She paused a short distance from the front door, studying the twin dragon statues that flanked the entrance. A tingle of magic rode across her skin. "This place is warded. I felt it when we came up the drive. Who would be stupid enough to take on the grand masters?"

"Unfortunately, there is an abundance of stupid in this world. And in Hell."

She couldn't argue with that. Conjuring up demons was complete lunacy, but somehow the necromancers never got that memo.

Riley climbed the stone steps, following Beck inside. The sound of footsteps came from a long arched hallway. The ancient guy who joined them had a wrinkled face and bright blue eyes. His thin build looked lost in the black turtleneck and slacks.

"Denver, welcome back," he said, his accent crisply English.

How cool. This place even has a butler.

"Riley, this is Grand Master Kepler. Sir, this is Riley Blackthorne."

Oops. Thank goodness she'd not said anything that would embarrass Beck. "Hi. I'm pleased to meet you," she said, politely.

Kepler briskly shook her hand, his grip surprisingly strong for one so aged. He held it a bit longer than was necessary, then let go. "It is a pleasure to meet you. Denver has told us much about you."

Probably not everything or you wouldn't be so nice to me.

"Riley will need her own room while she's here," Beck cut in. "We won't be sharin' one, not like I thought."

Riley gaped at him, caught completely off guard. Her boyfriend, had just thrown her under the bus in front of a grand master. And here she'd been worried about embarrassing him.

"I see," the older man said. "You can stay in the room next door to Denver's," he said. He shifted his eyes to Beck now. "The key is in the kitchen."

"Thank you, sir," Beck replied. He set off down the hallway, leaving her and the old master alone.

An understanding smile came her way. '*The course of true love never did run smooth,*' Kepler replied. "Not surprisingly, Shakespeare is still relevant today." He waved her on. "Come along, I'll show you where you need to go," he said.

Her anger still burning at being blindsided, Riley and the grand master walked down the hallway. Kepler took hold of her hand as if to steady himself. His grip was warm and reassuming.

The grand master gave her a sidelong glance. "When was the last time you were around a necromancer, Miss Blackthorne?"

"Ah, at the graveyard. Why?"

"Just curious," he replied.

Beck rejoined them at that moment, and she noted he wasn't meeting her eyes. "I'll take her from here, sir."

"Thank you. The stairs seem more daunting with each passing

year." Kepler turned toward Riley. "Have a peaceful stay, Miss Blackthorne."

"Thank you," she replied, touched by his kindness.

Beck hefted her small suitcase and led her up two long flights of oak stairs, an even grander version than those in Stewart's home. As they ascended, Riley's anger began to wane as she found herself staring in wonder at the portraits scattered along the walls.

She paused in front of one; the name plate stated this was Grand Master Jonathon P. Barnsbury, that he was from Aberdeen, and that he had lived from 1710-1783. Even more impressive – he was wearing a kilt.

"Will you get a portrait made some day?" she asked, intrigued.

Beck looked chagrined. "Yeah, I will. Part of the deal, I guess. Kinda freaks me out, you know?"

"I think it's way cool. Will you wear a kilt?"

"No," he replied flatly. "No way."

Riley paused in front of the next portrait – a lady named Antoinette LaFarge from Calais. "A woman. A French one. Now that rocks."

"There aren't many gals who've taken down a Fallen Angel, but if they do, they're one of us."

"So if I'd killed Sartael, I could have done all this," she replied thoughtfully. "I'm pretty envious here, just so you know."

Beck looked over at her, his expression softer now.

"In my mind, you're already one of us. You stood up to that bastard, and you have the scars to prove it. You've been to Hell and came back. There's little difference between you and me."

Of course there is. You never sold your soul.

Though Riley had expected something small, her room had a double bed as well as its own bathroom. The bedspread was a cheery rose color to match the thick curtains. An old desk sat under a broad multi-paned window, along with an electric tea kettle, tea supplies and a cup and saucer.

"It's nice," she said.

"Not bad," Beck replied as he unlocked the door between their two rooms. On impulse, she followed him into his space. His desk was piled high with leather bound books, proving that the guy who once had trouble reading was now a bookworm. Or at least an industrious student.

Stepping forward, she peered out the window onto a broad open vista which culminated at the edge of a forest. A narrow trail cut through the trees, angling up the tall hill behind the manor house.

"The loch is just over that hill," Beck explained. "I take my mornin' run that way. About killed me the first few times until I figured out I had to lighten my backpack cuz of the altitude."

"And now?"

"I'm up to forty pounds. I'm aimin' for fifty before I come back home."

Always pushing yourself.

"I wish I had this view back in Atlanta," she admitted. When Riley turned she found Beck close now. So close she could see deep into his eyes.

"Why did you tell Grand Master Kepler I needed my own room?"

His expression hardened. "I figured we both need some space right now."

"But you made that decision without asking me, without thinking how embarrassed I'd feel when you blurted that out."

He shrugged, which didn't earn him any points.

"You know, I'm done apologizing to you, Den. It isn't helping you're acting like a butthead and–."

He waved her to silence. "MacTavish wants to talk to you in the library. Best not to keep him waitin'."

"Oh, we'd hate to have that, wouldn't we?" she said, angry at the way he'd blown her off.

Though it was childish, Riley took her time unpacking, then joined Beck in the hallway. From the glower on his face, she'd pushed more than a few of his buttons.

Two can play that game, Backwoods Boy.

Despite all the drama, MacTavish wasn't waiting for them in the library. Riley barely noticed as she gasped the moment she stepped inside the room. It was like a Victorian dream come true; two stories tall with circular iron stairways that led to a second floor catwalk. A small dome rose in the very center of the ceiling, shedding soft light beneath it. Tables and padded chairs sat in discreet niches to allow for privacy. Reading lamps were dotted here and there, most with ornate stained glass shades. A fireplace sat at one end of the room, cozy flames warming the space. The room smelled of old paper and readily available knowledge. Just inhaling the scent seemed to ease some of the ache in her heart.

"Can I just move in here? This is like heaven."

"I figured you'd see it that way," Beck said. He waved her to one wall. "These are the ones you shouldn't touch," he said, indicating three shelves of books. Some were so old their bindings were cracked.

Now he had piqued her curiosity and Riley moved closer. "What keeps me from reading one of these when no one is looking?"

He gave her a hard stare.

"I'm just curious. Don't worry, I'm not going to do it."

"The books won't allow you ta touch them," MacTavish said, entering the room. He was smiling as he approached, dressed in comfortable slacks and a navy sweater. "Go ahead, try ta take one off the shelf."

Riley hesitated. "Is it going to fry me or something?"

"No, though ya'd regret it, and never feel the need ta do it again."

She shook her head. "I'll pass."

"No curiosity?" he teased.

"Sure, but sometimes curiosity costs too much," she said. "Besides, if I figure out all the mysteries in the world, then what?"

That earned her a chuckle from the grand master.

He and Beck traded looks, an unspoken message passed.

"I'll ... catch up with you later," Beck said, then left them alone.

The grand master found himself a chair near the fire.

"Feel free ta look around," he said, gesturing.

Why not? MacTavish was a bit like Angus Stewart, so he'd get down to business when it suited him. Riley took herself went on a tour of the shelves. The books were in various languages, including Latin, Greek, Russian and German. Something for everyone.

"If yer lookin' for family histories, the records are there," the Scotsman said, pointing toward the opposite wall. "There'll be somethin' on the Blackthornes."

She turned toward him, surprised. "Why? None of my people were grand masters, at least I don't think so."

"No, but they were instrumental in establishin' the Demon Trappers in England. Ya've a rich history, lass."

Riley sighed in frustration. "My dad never told me much. He really didn't want me to be a trapper."

"Not surprisin'. As ya well ken, it's a hard life," the man replied.

"That's the truth." *It's cost me the guy I love.*

With a little hunting, Riley found her family's history, all *five* volumes' worth. The final one was a looseleaf binder whose contents began in 1979 and ran through current day. She flipped it open, read a few lines and then jerked her head up. "I'm in here."

"Of course ya are, lass," MacTavish replied. "Master Kepler keeps the records up-ta-date. Once we have enough information, we have the manuscript properly typeset and bound. It'll be a few years before that happens ta the one yer holdin'." He gestured. "If anythin' needs correctin', let me know."

"I will, thanks." She still couldn't quite wrap her head around the fact that someone cared enough to record the history of *her* family.

"I hear ya turned down Beck's proposal," MacTavish said, as if he had a right to talk about something that personal. "May I ask why?"

Riley frowned, growing irritated. "With all respect, I don't think that's your business, sir."

"It is when it affects one of our people," he replied, his voice taking on a sharper edge. "Denver is verra much in love with ya. I had thought the feelin' was reciprocated. Now he tells me it's not. That makes me curious as ta what has changed."

Riley knew he wasn't going to back down, so she gave in.

"I just..." Once again she tried to get a handle on her turbulent emotions, which seemed to see-saw back and forth without warning.

"Lass?" he nudged.

She chose a chair near him and the fire, slumping down into it, still holding the binder. "Honest, I don't know. I just ... One minute I want to be with him forever and then next I don't ... trust him."

"It's it only him ya don't trust?"

"No. I have trouble trusting anyone. I feel like I should be running away, that someone is after me. It's ... weird." She rubbed her temple, as if that could make things right.

"Headache?" MacTavish asked.

"Sort of. I have this hum in my brain all the time now. It's hard to think."

"When did it start?"

"Ah ... a couple days ago. It's just jet lag."

MacTavish's brow furrowed. "Aye, that's probably it."

She needed to change the subject. "How is Bess' daughter? Is she still really sick?"

He nodded. "Kepler thinks she's dyin' because she's been bespelled."

"What? Why would someone do that to a kid?" Then it made sense. "Because it made her mom agree to kidnap me, to get me to that graveyard as demon bait."

"That's what we think."

"Whoever did this is evil."

"Aye." He rose, watching her carefully. "I have only one more question; if Beck had asked ya ta marry him at the graveyard, would ya have said aye?"

"Of course," she replied, without thinking. Riley began twisting the ring on her right hand with her thumb. "I love him so very much."

"But not now."

"I don't know," she replied, more confused than ever.

"Who knows, perhaps he'll ask ya again."

"He won't," she said, feeling the certainty of those words and how bitter they tasted. "Den has his pride, and I've hurt him ... badly."

"Well, at least ya see that. I'll leave ya ta it then. I hope ya find our house peaceful, Ms. Blackthorne."

Grand Master MacTavish departed, quietly closing the door behind him. As if by magic, Riley's eyes strayed to the section of forbidden books. Then she shook her head.

Not going there.

After thumbing through the binder's contents, she read about her father, how he'd come from a long line of English trappers and how he'd been recruited by Master Angus Stewart. Some of that she knew, other parts provided revelations. There were a few notes about Riley's mom and then details about her dad's most notable demon captures. One, in particular, proved difficult to read; the night her father had tangled with an Archfiend and lost his soul. That revelation had been slotted in on an extra page, because at the time no one had known he'd made a deal with Hell.

"All for me." Such deep love was almost more than she could bear.

The longer she read about her dad and the Blackthornes, the words seemed to calm the buzz in her mind. Unfortunately, they did nothing for the void in her heart. Only Beck could fill that.

As time passed, the silence of the library did bring that peace the masters spoke of. Reluctantly, Riley re-shelved the binder and then returned to the fire, the room chillier than she would have liked.

"Why did everything go wrong?" she muttered. Now that she thought it through, her attitude toward Beck had changed when she'd arrived at the hotel. Before that, she was fine, but once she was in that room, she'd gone from relief that he'd been at her side, to wanting him gone.

The *why* proved elusive. A current heart check told her she still loved him, despite his recent behavior, and that her distrust of him was minimal. Did it have something to do with the manor house?

Their wards?

If Bess' daughter had been bespelled, why not her? No, that didn't track. Like she'd told Kepler, she hadn't been near a necromancer since the graveyard.

Feeling frustrated, Riley's attention wandered to the forbidden books and she eyed them much like a kid in a candy shop. It was tempting as the titles promised hidden knowledge in necromancy, demonology and arcane magic. Maybe the answer is in one of those book, and if she found it…

"No." She just couldn't go there, not after all the grand masters had done for her and Beck.

She headed toward a computer tucked in a corner on a small oak table. When she jiggled the mouse, the monitor lit up and promptly asked for a password. She frowned, then remembered she'd seen it on a sticky note on Beck's desk. Fortunately it was memorable enough that she typed it in.

It took some time to compose the e-mail to Mort, mostly because it was full of heartbreak. If she hadn't known him so well, she wouldn't be exposing herself like this. Once she'd covered the horrific details, she moved into the questions.

What are the ways a summoner can put a spell on a person? Can the spell be done long distance? If so, how would they keep it going? Is it possible someone has cast a spell on me to make me so paranoid?

I swear, I would never have turned down Beck's proposal if I'd been home in Atlanta.

PLEASE HELP ME!

She hit Send. "Come on, Mort. Tell me what's really going on. Tell me I'm not going crazy."

Riley logged out and leaned back in the chair, her arms crossed over her chest. A lengthy yawn told her give it up and go have a nap. Maybe by the time she awoke Mort would have replied with something that helped her make sense of her screwed up life.

A fresh bottle of Holy Water sat in front of her door, courtesy of Brennan. Once inside, she set the bottle on the floor and booted up her computer. When she went to check her e-mail, just in case Mort had already replied, the password didn't work.

Muttering under her breath, she tapped on the door that led to Beck's room and that got her a gruff "Yeah?"

Riley creaked the door open and peered inside. Beck was at his desk, books open all around him, but he appeared distracted.

"The password's not working. Is there a new one now?"

He nodded and fished around in the top drawer for a piece of paper. "It changes every day at three in the afternoon, for security."

Their fingers touched when he handed over the paper and she found herself peering down into pair of exhausted brown eyes.

"Are we okay?" she asked.

A half-hearted shrug was his reply as a slight frown creased his forehead. "Not sure. How are you doin'?"

When she hesitated, he rose, stepping closer. "Don't lie. Just tell me how you feel. Happy? Sad? What?"

"I'm empty inside, like I've lost something important." *You.*

Beck cocked his head. "Same here. What's goin' on between us doesn't feel right. I mean ... it's not like us."

"Like me, you mean. I'm the one who suddenly went bizarre."

Beck nodded, then opened up his arms. Without hesitation, she walked into them, surrendering to the embrace, wondering how she could ever live without this guy.

"That's better," he murmured near her ear. "You've been too distant the last couple of days."

She laid her head on his chest. "I wrote Mort and asked him to help us. I need to know what's happening with me. I want things the way they used to be." *The way they should be.*

"Same here," he said.

He raised her head and then gently kissed her. Warmth spread through her body.

"I should let you study," she murmured after the second kiss.

"Yeah," he replied, bending in for another.

Finally, she broke away, unsure of going any further than just kissing. Too much was in flux right now.

"Oh, we got a supper thing going on tonight. You'll need to dress up. It's kinda fancy," he said.

"Okay." There really wasn't much else she could say.

"So you know, it's not just us tonight." Beck looked away, as if he was about to tell her something she wouldn't like. "Summoner Fayne will be here – she's one of the mid-level necros, from what I hear. Monsignor Lang and Archdruid Scrimshaw will be here too."

"After what happened to me, they invited a summoner to dinner? Are they crazy?" she demanded.

"It's a MacTavish thing," Beck replied. "He likes to keep an eye on folks. Figures the best way to do that is to talk to them every now and then. Who knows, maybe we'll learn something by havin' one of their kind here for chow."

Riley drew back. "Well, that whole idea just sucks. Do I really have to be there?"

"Yeah. Sorry."

She swore under her breath. "Then do me a favor – keep the necro *away* from me. I don't want to lose it front of everyone."

Beck grinned. "Now that's the Riley I remember. Dinner's at seven."

"Good. I need a nap." Maybe that way she'd be less inclined to commit necro-cide over dessert.

Chapter Eight

The shower brought Riley back to life, and after mussing with her hair and makeup, she tugged on a pair of heavy tights, then her new dress from the secondhand shop. It was soft emerald green wool and its hem ended just a few inches above her knees. Its long sleeves were a prudent choice as the manor was drafty. Even better, it fit her perfectly, its color doing lovely things for her complexion. Riley tugged the zipper up and adjusted the neckline and then put on the earrings Beck had bought her in Edinburgh.

She did a twirl in front of the mirror. *Hey, look at me!*

Now it was time to show off her off new outfit.

"Den... ?" she asked, walking into his room unannounced. "What do you think? Will this be okay?"

Beck stuck his head out of the bathroom, nervously adjusting a black bow tie. His eyes widened as he took her in. "You look so pretty."

Which was exactly what she'd hoped he say.

Riley gave him a huge smile, which faltered the instant he stepped out of the bathroom. Besides the bow tie, he was wearing a fancy dress shirt and black waistcoat, topped by a black Bonnie Prince Charlie jacket. The kind Stewart wore on special occasions. But that wasn't all.

He was wearing a kilt.

Her mouth dropped open in astonishment.

The kilt was made of fine red and black wool and he had the little extras to complete the outfit: the *sporran*, the flashes, and the *sgian dubh*, the short knife stuck in one of his knee-highs. His black shoes were highly polished.

Beck turned toward her, his expression worried. "What do you think? Do I look stupid?"

"Oh wow, I mean… " Riley said. "You're…" *So hot.*

"I look like a dork, don't I? I was afraid of that," Beck said, nervously tugging on the jacket now.

"You do *not* look like a dork," Riley replied, moving closer. "You're…" She took a deep breath to keep her mind from veering off into some seriously steamy fantasies, all of which involved them missing supper entirely.

Riley cupped his face, inhaling his aftershave. "I thought you were awesome before, but now you're just…" She sighed. "You are sooo handsome, Den."

He blinked in surprise, as if the idea had never crossed his mind. "Yer sure? I can wear somethin' else."

"No! You're wearing that kilt. You are totally hot." *Scorching even.* "Do we really have to go downstairs?"

"Yeah," he said, shaking his head. "I know, but we have no choice. MacTavish wants our guests to meet me. And you, too."

"Ohhhkay. Hold on, your tie's crooked. Let me fix it for you."

As she adjusted it, he relaxed even further.

"The tartan is from the Macpherson clan," he explained. "Figured I should honor my gran's people."

Riley touched his cheek again. "You're a really cool guy."

"You know, maybe I shoulda worn this up on Arthur's Seat," he said. "Might have got a different answer."

She winced and stepped back, putting distance between them. Whether it was on purpose or not, he'd ruined the moment with a reminder of just how bad she'd hurt him. Even if they did get married some day, would he always hold that one mistake over her head?

"We should be going," she said, turning away, trying not to let the hurt show on her face.

"Riley," he began, catching her arm. "God, I'm sorry. I shouldn't have said that."

Then why did you?

~ ~ ~ ~ ~

The druid was a middle-aged woman with bright red hair and a big smile. When Mrs. Scrimshaw took hold of Riley hand, it felt like the lady had offloaded a bunch of "feel good" pheromones.

"I'm so pleased to meet you," Scrimshaw said, her accent neither English or Scottish. At Riley's puzzled look, she added, "I'm Canadian."

"Ah, got it. I hated to ask, you know?"

"I get that all the time." Mrs. Scrimshaw turned to Beck, took in the full kilted package and beamed. "Well, grand masters are looking better every day. I'm *very* pleased to meet you, Mr. Beck."

"Thank you, ma'am."

Monsignor Lang greeted Riley politely, but he skipped the handshake. Besides that standard clerical garb, he had a luxuriant moustache and solemn brown eyes.

Did he know that she'd been grilled by the Vatican's Demon Hunters? Or her involvement with a certain Fallen angel? There was no good way to ask those questions, so Riley just smiled in return.

"It is a pleasure to meet you, Miss Blackthorne," Lang said. "I recently spoke with a friend of yours, a young man named Simon Adler."

"Simon?" she said, surprised, looking over at Beck and then back to the priest. "He's here in Scotland?" Lang nodded. "How is he? I haven't gotten an e-mail from him for a while." Which wasn't unusual for her ex-boyfriend, so she hadn't been terribly worried.

"He's doing fairly well. I spoke with him about a month ago. He indicated that a period of contemplative prayer will be beneficial, so I made arrangements for him to go to Pluscarden Abbey, for a retreat. It's a Benedictine monastery in northern Scotland. From what I gather, he's still there."

"Good, he'll like that. I'm glad for him," she said, meaning every word. "How did you meet him?" *And why did he mention me?*

"A representative of the Vatican asked if I could help Mr. Adler while he was here."

The Vatican? Now *that* was interesting.

"Thanks for helping him. Simon's a good guy."

"Yeah, he is," Beck said softly. "Hell was *really* hard on him."

"It is on all of us," the monsignor replied. His eyes moved back to Riley. "Some more than most."

Riley intended to follow up on that comment, but was interrupted by someone calling out her name. She gritted her teeth. Not willing to risk offending the grand masters in any way, she reluctantly turned toward the approaching necromancer.

Fayne was in her mid-fifties, with dark hair and full lips, wearing a dark brown robe. She frankly assessed Riley like a jeweler would a rare diamond.

Biting the inside of her lip, Riley put on her "I'm here only because I have to be, so don't push your luck" expression.

When the summoner offered to shake her hand, Beck intervened.

"Good to meet you, ma'am," he said, intercepting the woman's handshake. "I'm Denver Beck."

"The new grand master?" she asked, studying him closely.

"Not yet, ma'am. I'm still workin' toward that. It's a long haul."

"*You* actually killed an angel?" the woman asked, skepticism overlaying each word.

Her tone made Riley's hackles rise.

"It was either that or it'd kill me," Beck replied.

Fayne's attention moved back to Riley and she stretched out her hand again.

Riley ignored it. Before it became even more awkward, Kepler interceded, guiding Fayne across the room to meet the druid. From the look on the necro's face, she wasn't pleased by the interruption.

"If it wasn't for Mort, I'd never talk to another summoner again," Riley murmured.

"Same here," Beck agreed. "Since Simon's in Scotland, I'll try to catch up with him if I can. Buy him a beer. See how things are goin'."

"If you do talk to him, tell him I'm thinking of him," she replied.

"I will. Funny thing, down the line I'll be spending some time at that monastery too."

Riley blinked. "Why?"

"It's during the last few weeks of a grand master's trainin'. Kepler says that by then I'll need some quiet time to work things out in my head."

"You? In a monastery? That outta be fun," she said, rolling her eyes.

Beck frowned back. "A few months ago, I wouldn't have done it. Now?" He nodded more to himself than her. "I think I'll like it. It'll be straightforward. So much of my life isn't that way anymore."

"You really have changed," she said, looking up at him.

"Not so much on the outside," he said.

She pointed at the kilt and he shrugged in acceptance.

"Well, maybe so." Then his eyes slowly rose to meet hers. "Do you ... like ... the new me?"

There was so much turbulent emotion behind the question it drowned out everything around them.

"It's taking a bit to get used to, but I do like the new Beck. I'm so proud of you," she said.

He took her hand and kissed it. "Then there is still a chance for us?"

"I think so, if I can get my head straightened out."

"Good." He dropped a kiss on her cheek and then smiled. "Then let's get this supper over with, so it's just us two, okay?"

Riley's cheeks warmed at what his husky tone implied.

After more social chitchat among the guests, which carefully avoided the twin minefields of politics and religion, the group headed for the formal dining room. It was spacious, and sported two fireplaces, one on each end of the long room. Unfortunately the majority of the heat headed directly toward the high ceiling and Riley's feet and ankles didn't like that.

As she gazed around, she realized the dining room sent two opposing messages: the long table was set with expensive bone china, elegant crystal and silverware, a fine welcome to any guest. In contrast, the walls were lined with swords and other implements of war, many arrayed in intricate fan shapes. It was a not-so-subtle reminder that their hosts could easily shift from hospitable, to lethal, if the situation warranted.

Walk softly and carry a really big sword.

She shot a look at Beck and he nodded ever so slightly to indicate he'd gotten the message as well. Since this evening, they'd been on the same wavelength, more like they had been in Atlanta. Riley prayed that would continue.

Her good mood vanished when Riley found herself seated across from the summoner, who continued to stare at her. MacTavish sat at the head of the table, Kepler to his right and Beck to his left. There was a light sheen of sweat on Beck's forehead, his way of showing he was nervous. She gave him a reassuring *you'll do fine* look and then directed her attention to the conversation around her.

Around them, Brennan and the maid circulated with bottles of wine. When he gave her a questioning look, Riley shook her head. Even though she could legally drink in this country, her mind was just starting to clear. No reason to mess it up again.

Some sort of thick and creamy pale orange soup was delivered and her stomach growled in response. Fortunately no one else heard it. Picking up a spoon, she looked down the table at Beck, who was staring at his assortment of silverware in total bewilderment.

MacTavish said something to the druid, then pointedly picked up the proper spoon from his selection. Beck, ever the quick study, followed suit, then looked over at her.

She winked and addressed the meal.

"Miss Blackthorne? I trust you are recovered from the incident at the graveyard?" the summoner asked, lobbing the question across the table like a live grenade.

Riley nearly choked on her soup. She hadn't expected anyone would ask that kind of question, especially here. Farther down the table, Brennan's eyes widened as he refilled a wine glass. Beck's brow furrowed and she could tell he was pissed.

MacTavish, however, made no move to deflect the question. Perhaps he was hoping just this kind of confrontation would occur.

Play dumb. That was the best response, especially with the monsignor at the table. The last thing she needed was for the Vatican to take a renewed interest in her life.

Riley hedged. "I'm sorry, I don't know what you mean," she replied.

"Of course you do," Fayne insisted. "My superiors told me everything."

"Your superiors?" Beck cut in.

"Summoners Enfield and Minton. They were supposed to be here tonight, but I requested to take their place. I just had to meet Miss Blackthorne after everything I'd heard."

"What exactly happened?" the monsignor said after wiping his mouth with a napkin.

Riley kept her groan of despair to herself.

"Someone tried to summon a demon in Edinburgh and it went wrong." Fayne's chilly tone indicated she wasn't that concerned, even though three people had died. "Novices. Such things happen when they are involved."

The monsignor's moustache twitched in response. "It could be argued that *no one* should be attempting such things, amateur or expert," he weighed in, his eyes on Riley now.

"I totally agree," she said.

Fayne turned back toward her, eyes cagey. "Why do you think the summoning went wrong?"

"I'm not the one you should ask. I'm a Demon Trapper. I don't do magic."

"That's not what I heard." Fayne retorted.

She glared at the necromancer. "Then whoever is telling you this stuff is full of it."

"Riley," Grand Master Kepler cut in. "Is it true that you are compiling the history of Atlanta's trappers for Grand Master Stewart?"

She sighed in relief. *Thank you, dude. I owe you one.*

"Yes, sir. It's been really interesting. There was more demonic activity during the Civil War than I thought."

"Hellspawn working for Sherman? I just can't believe it," Beck said, his tone mocking. "I mean, it's not like the general turned a couple of Pyro-Fiends loose to burn Atlanta down or anythin'." He paused, timing it perfectly. "Oh wait..."

That earned him some laughs, and, more importantly, shut down the summoner's mini inquisition.

Beck caught her eye and it was his turn to wink. They were a team again and that felt so good.

What the hell am I doin' here? Beck didn't know a thing about this kind of get together. For him, barbecue and beer was fancy.

MacTavish picked up the farthest fork from the left and then gestured with it toward the plate that had just been placed in front of Beck.

"Looks to be a fine bit of lamb," he said.

In his own way, the grand master was helping him navigate these uncharted waters. Helping him grow into his new skin. Beck carefully selected the proper fork from his numerous choices and began working on the food.

Though the point of the dinner seemed to be social, MacTavish and Kepler were strategists, just like Stewart. It came with being a Grand Master.

So why do they have that necro here? Why is she pushing Riley so hard? Did she have somethin' to do with what happened in the graveyard?

At this point Riley laughed at a remark from the druid, and Beck smiled to himself. He never quite understood how her voice could be a balm to him, but it was. Looking at her now, you'd never know she'd been to Hell and back.

Maybe, if things kept getting better between them, he'd find the courage to ask his question again.

Maybe the next time she'd say "yes."

Chapter Nine

Once the guests were gone, Riley and Beck joined the two masters in a cozy sitting room. She snuggled next to her guy on a leather sofa, utilizing Beck's furnace feature to warm herself. As much as she loved Scotland, she really missed Atlanta's warmer climate.

MacTavish lit a pipe, filling the air with a rich caramel aroma. That reminded her of Master Stewart, how every evening they'd share how their day went. She missed him, wished he was here. *He'd know how to make things right again.*

After light talk about the dinner and the guests, the topic of conversation turned to business.

"According to Summoner Fayne's superiors," Kepler began, "they have not been able to find out what where that demonic spell originated. In short, the necromancers have closed ranks."

"Figured that might happen. But wouldn't there be some sort of magical trace left behind?" Beck said.

"They claim there wasn't one."

"That's a lie," Riley said. "Our friend Mortimer – he's a summoner – said that each necro has their own 'magical signature.'"

"Your friend is correct," Kepler said, nodding.

MacTavish cleared his throat. "Riley, would ya give us a chance ta talk this out ... in private?"

She was being dismissed? "I have as much at stake in this as you guys do."

"Aye, but right now ya need trust us," he replied.

Riley shot to her feet. "Okay, I'll just go to my room and buff my nails while you guys can talk state secrets. Will that work for you?"

"Riley..." Beck murmured, shaking his head in dismay.

"We'll talk more in the mornin'," MacTavish replied. "Good night, lass."

Riley resisted the urge to slam the door behind her as fury propelled her down the hall and then up the staircase.

Will it always be like this?

If she and Beck kept secrets from each other now, over the years that cancer would spread, poisoning their relationship. First he wouldn't tell her about his work, then it'd be other things; who he'd talked to or met for a drink or...

But if I want to be part of his life, this is what I have to do.

In her room, she kicked off her shoes and changed into her jeans and a long-sleeved tee shirt. Thick, fluffy socks came next and they soothed her cold feet.

The rowdy part of her insisted she go back downstairs. The unsure part of her didn't want to act like some little girl begging for an invitation into the big boy's tree house.

As her temper gradually cooled, Riley checked her e-mails and found there wasn't much new in Atlanta, which was reassuring. Beck's neighbor, Mrs. Morton, had left a short note to report that his house and bunny rabbit were both in fine shape. And Riley's Latin assignment for the week had been posted online.

Mort's reply wasn't comforting. In a few succinct paragraphs he explained how it was possible for a summoner to influence another's behavior, how the magic user didn't need to be in the presence of the victim, only that the compulsion spell was replenished every now and then.

Her contact with summoners had been limited, at least until tonight, which meant that all her confusion probably wasn't caused by a spell. More likely it was a fundamental flaw with her and Beck's relationship.

She felt her eyes misting.

I can't lose him now. Not like this.

A tap came at her door. Confused as to who this might be, Riley opened it to find the maid with a tray in hand. "Excuse me, Miss. Thought you might like some hot cocoa."

"Thanks," Riley said and accepted the tray. The young girl retreated down the hall as she toed the door closed.

Beck had probably arranged the delivery as a peace offering, trying to make amends.

Note to self: stop being a butthead. At least to Beck.

Sinking back into the desk chair, Riley picked up the cup, savoring the heady scent of dark chocolate. Right before she took a sip, she read further into the e-mail.

'Spells can be laid on food and liquids in such a way that the victim will have no idea they are being enchanted. It's old tech, but it does work quite effectively.'

"Liquids?" she murmured. Then peered down at the cup. How did she know that there wasn't something in the drink? Or what about the shortbread cookies that accompanied the hot chocolate? Or if she was really going to be paranoid, why not in the water she'd had at supper?

I'm driving myself crazy.

After three unsuccessful tries to let the cup touch her lips, Riley reluctantly dumped the delicious drink down the bathroom sink and rinsed out the cup. Staring up in the mirror revealed the underlying weariness that seemed to age her from within.

Riley pushed her hair off her face, then growled under her breath. Paul Blackthorne's daughter should be down there with the grand masters, not cowering in her room. Beck would be angry at her for barging into the meeting, but she didn't care. Steeling herself, she let the door slip closed behind her and headed toward the stairs.

Beck's loyalties were badly divided: he wanted to listen to the conversation between the two masters, maybe learn more about what was happening with Riley, but the other part of him was worried about her. He'd seen the look on her face, how angry she was at being sent away. She'd never tolerated being treated like a nuisance, and he suspected that anger would be directed at him just when they were starting to mend fences.

"Look, I know you think yer doin' what's best for her, but I know Riley. She's got a right to be here."

"We're not includin' her because we're not sure just how compromised she is," MacTavish explained.

"I don't understand. What do you mean ... compromised?"

Kepler's aged hands knotted together in his lap. "I have a bit of magical ability myself, and I sensed an enchantment when Riley walked in the front door this morning. Your young lady is under a necromancer's spell."

"What?" Beck replied, caught off guard. "But..." Then it made sense. "All this paranoia stuff. You think someone's made her that way?" *Please God, let it be that.*

"I'm sure of it," Kepler said.

"So who did it to her?" he demanded, his fists clenched now. "Was it that summoner you had at dinner tonight?"

Kepler looked over at MacTavish. "Yes, it was."

"What!?" Beck launched to his feet. "And you let her go?"

MacTavish waved him back into his chair and Beck reluctantly complied.

"We let her go free because we don't have enough evidence against her. We arranged it so she was here tonight so Kepler could feel out her magic. Now that we know she's involved, we can take the matter before her superiors."

"They're not gonna do a damned thing. Why the hell didn't we just nail her to the wall?"

"Trust me, I woulda loved ta have sliced off her head and sent it as a warnin' ta those damned meddlin' fools, but sometimes ya have ta see the bigger picture."

"There is nothing more important than Riley's safety," Beck said. The moment he said the words, he felt the indecision. As a grand master he couldn't be that way, couldn't limit his world to just one person.

Or could he?

"I don't know if I can do this," he admitted. "All the learnin' and such, that's been okay. But this ... damn ... I feel like I'm bein' ripped apart."

MacTavish gave a solemn nod. "If ya weren't, we'd be worried. We all went through this, each one of us in our way. We had ta find peace within ourselves, negotiate the balance between our personal lives and our mission."

Silence fell, each of them caught in private thoughts.

Was this the way it would always be for him, stuck between the grand masters and the woman he loved?

Beck slowly unclenched his fists and allowed his arms to fall free on either side of the chair. He took a deep breath and let it out slowly.

MacTavish nodded his approval. "I know it's hard, lad, and it never gets easier. Especially when ya love someone so verra much."

"So what is this bigger picture yer talkin' about?"

"This isn't the first time the necros have been pokin' around in Hell. Our biggest worry is if they will ally with Lucifer. By goin' slowly, we can keep the other necros on the straight and narrow, while dealin' with the immediate problem."

Beck stilled. "Then why didn't ya tell Riley all this?"

"I'm concerned that if Fayne learns we're onto her," Kepler said, "she may well compel Riley to harm herself. No living witness? No charges."

"Ah, shit," Beck murmured. "I never thought of that." He rubbed a hand over this face. "I knew somethin' was wrong. Riley stopped trustin' me, and that's not like her. We've been through so much together, for her to just back off..."

"That's why I knew somethin' was up," MacTavish said. "Neither of ya are lightweights when it comes ta hard times. The moment ya came back from Hell, we had ta know everythin' about ya. Even yer private life."

"Riley's not part of this," Beck said, though he knew that wasn't the truth.

"She's as much a part of who ya are as anyone," MacTavish retorted. "Ya've been readin' our history – Hell works through all channels ta destroy us. What better way than corruptin' one of yer own family?" MacTavish took a deep breath to calm himself.

"That's why we were so pleased that ya'd found a lass who knew what ya were facin', knew Hell's tricks, had even beaten them at their own game."

"Without a strong force in your life, it's too easy to be tempted," Kepler explained. He and MacTavish exchanged a solemn look.

"Been there?" Beck asked softly.

"Aye. All of us have, at one time or another," MacTavish replied.

Beck frowned. "I should check on Riley. Make sure she's okay."

"Tell her we'll talk over breakfast, lay it all out for her. Then I'll contact Fayne's superiors."

Beck nodded and rose. He'd taken only a few steps toward the door when the maid scurried in, her face white.

"Sirs..."

"What's wrong?" Beck said, taking a step closer. "Is Riley okay?"

"I was headed to the kitchen and ... and ... I saw her with Mr. Brennan. They were going out the side door. He had a knife at her throat."

"Oh, sweet Jesus!" Beck exclaimed, and took off a run.

Chapter Ten

"That's right. Just keep moving."

Riley was outdoors, Brennan holding tight to her arm. In his other hand was a knife, the one that had convinced her to not fight him, at least not yet.

It'd been her fault; she really hadn't been paying attention when he'd had accosted her in the downstairs hall. Now she cursed herself for not sensing the danger before he'd pulled the knife and told her to keep silent.

As they climbed the hill behind the manor house her mind raced with questions. How had she misread this guy all along?

Riley wasn't wearing a coat or gloves and the crisp night air cut into her, her teeth chattering in response to the cold. There was a slight breeze as the clouds moved across the moon, alternately obscuring and then revealing its pale glow. It felt like snow was in the air.

She knew that calling out for help wasn't an option - no one would hear her out here. "Why are you doing this?" Riley demanded.

"Because she'll help me get what I want," was the terse reply, the knife never wavering.

"She?"

"Fayne," he said, sounding as if the word tasted sour.

"You have to be kidding me." The grand masters had dined with her kidnapper and never known it. Or had they? Was this one big scheme or...

"Did MacTavish know she was behind this?"

Brennan gave her quick frown. "No, I don't think so, but you never know with him. He's a cagey old bird."

As they climbed, shrubs tugging on her jeans, Riley felt magic build around them, the same dark magic that had been in the graveyard. Things began to come clear.

"She put a spell on me, didn't she? That's why I was so weird to Beck."

"Yes. It was in the Holy Water I gave you."

"What? Damn you!" she said, trying to pull herself out of his grip, but failing. "You ruined my life!"

"That wasn't the intention," he replied. "I just wanted..."

She glared at him. "Wanted what?"

"Nobody was supposed to die," he said, his voice trembling now. "It went all wrong."

"Really. And Bess' little girl? What about her?"

Her captor shook his head. "I didn't know Fayne put a spell on the kid until later. I was just supposed to make sure Robbie picked you up at the airport instead of Beck."

More pieces of the puzzle dropped in place. "You did something to make Beck sick, didn't you?"

"Yeah. I put some stuff in his oatmeal. It didn't hurt him."

They skirted around a broad patch of heather as their breath clouded the night air.

Riley snorted. "I guess throwing up for a few hours is no big deal in your world."

Brennan's hand tightened on her arm, digging into her flesh. "He's okay now. It's not like I wanted to hurt him. He's been decent to me."

"Then why do all this?"

"I want to be a grand master," he replied, his eyes flashing at her. "Fayne will summon a Fallen and then I'll kill it. They'll have to let me become one of them."

Riley came to abrupt halt, forcing Brennan to stop. "Are you crazy? Do you have any idea how evil those things are?"

"You're just like MacTavish," he snapped, frowning again. "He only wants his favorites to become a grand master."

"What? It doesn't ... work that way. It's not like some popularity contest," she said, her teeth chattering harder now. He tugged her along and they resumed the climb. "Look, we can go back to the house, explain what happened to you and–"

"Just keep walking," he said.

She wasn't getting through to him.

"So why do the summoning in the graveyard? What did that buy you guys?"

"Fayne wanted to test the elements of the spell, make sure they were right before she tried to summon a Fallen. Robbie was all over that, eager to impress her, I guess."

"Yeah, that really worked for him."

When she crested the hill, out of breath and body quaking, Riley forced herself to look over her shoulder. To her relief, the manor house had more lights on now. Did they realize she was gone? Or was it nothing more than the others getting ready for bed?

Beck will find me. He'll know something's wrong.

But maybe she could give him a bit of help. If she could get back to the manor...

Riley swung around and kicked at Brennan's closest knee, dropping him to the ground with a cry. Rather than try to wrestle the knife from him, she took off down the hill, veering around stones. She'd covered only a short distance when a voice boomed in her head, clamping onto her will with steel claws.

"Come to me!" the voice ordered, causing her to skid to a stop. Though she tried to fight the spell, Riley turned like a puppet and continued on, past Brennan, to the crown of the hill.

Her captor swore as he caught up with her, but made no attempt to restrain her. He didn't need to – his "boss" was pulling her strings.

They walked along the crown of the ridge, the loch to their left, until a bonfire became visible along a flat stretch of ground dotted with heather and stones. Summoner Fayne stood by the fire, her dark brown robe nearly making her invisible in the darkness.

"Come closer," the summoner said, beckoning.

Riley's mind told to submit, that it was useless to resist such power. Her heart told her if she did, she was dead.

Brennan limped closer now, looking anxiously back and forth between Riley and the necromancer. "This damn well better work," he muttered, shaking his head in dismay.

"All will go smoothly," Fayne replied.

"It didn't go smoothly for Robbie and the others," Riley cut in. "They're dead."

"Their blood is on your hands, not mine," the summoner retorted. "If you had not fought back, the demon would have been happy just to kill you, not them."

"No, that's not how it was," Riley said, her memories conjuring up the horrific images of the dead summoners. Of Bess weeping in terror. "You knew Robbie couldn't hold that Archfiend. He didn't have enough power."

Fayne ignored that. "Sit there," the woman ordered, pointing toward a bare patch of ground. Riley moved to the spot she'd indicated, forced to comply so her head wouldn't explode from the pressure. The instant her butt hit the hard ground she went into another long shivering session. It was so cold, she could barely feel the tips of her fingers.

Beck, where are you?

Fayne was closer now, the magic rolling off her in waves. She placed a ceremonial knife and a piece of paper on the ground within Riley's reach.

Riley glared up at her. "MacTavish and Beck will figure out I'm missing and come looking for me."

"Let them," the necromancer replied, her eyes alight. "They pose no threat. A few dead grand masters won't trouble me at all."

"Hey!" Brennan said, limping closer now. "That's not our deal. You are to summon the Fallen so I can kill it. You can't hurt the masters or I'm screwed."

The summoner laughed. "If they get in my way, they will be harmed. If you thought otherwise, you're an idiot."

"No! I won't let you hurt them."

"Then they'd best not challenge me."

"The necro is hosing you over," Riley said. "The only way she'll summon a Fallen is to kill me. How else will she get one of Lucifer's own this close to the grand master's stronghold?"

"No, you'll be fine," Brennan insisted, but he sounded unsure now. "We agreed that she would wipe your memory once it was over. I'll tell the masters I found you out here wandering around all confused. That I rescued you from the Fallen. I'll be the hero."

You are so naive.

With a bark of laughter, Fayne tossed a sword at his feet. As Brennan picked it up, his eyes met Riley's. "It'll be okay," he said, shooting a quick glance toward the necromancer as she returned to the fire. He lowered his voice. "I'll keep you safe, no matter what."

Riiight.

Fayne invoked her magical circle and it snapped into place with a burst of dark grey light, destined to protect her from one of Hell's most dangerous servants. Unlike Robbie's, this circle thrummed with power. Fayne may not be at Mort's level of magic, but she had enough expertise to do a lot of damage.

After a sharp intake of breath, as if realizing there was no going back, Brennan called out. "I'm ready."

Riley tried to rise, but the effort proved futile. The buzzing her mind was at hornet nest level now, making it hard to think. She had to buy time.

"If you summon a Fallen it's going to kill him," she said, angling her head toward the grand master wannabe, "and take you as its own."

Fayne sniffed in derision. "No Fallen will ever command me. It will be my servant."

"Why? What does this buy you?"

"Respect. None of the others think I am capable of such a thing, but after tonight they will know I am the most powerful summoner in all the world."

Now that's a planet-sized ego. Which was all Hell needed to work their own special brand of chaos.

Knowing she was wasting her time trying to talk sense into Fayne or Brennan, Riley shifted her attention to escape. When she tried to rise again, nothing happened other than making sweat stand out on her forehead and her head pound in time with her heart.

There's got to be a way to break free.

Fayne raised her head, almost like she was scenting the wind, and smiled. "The masters have realized you're missing and are hurrying to join us. What a merry party we will have."

That was good news. Or was it?

Maybe that had been Fayne's plan – to lure Beck and the others out of the safety of their house and end their lives at the hands of a Fallen.

Is she that smart? Or has Hell been playing her all along?

Unaware of Riley's inner dialog, Fayne began to chant, grayish-blue light swirling around her hands. Riley knew this spell – two months earlier she'd been with Mort on a summoning and this was similar. The deceased had been a young girl, just fourteen, and Mort had felt Riley's presence might be a comfort when the deceased rose from her grave. The experience had left Riley heartbroken, vowing never to be involved in that kind of thing again, even though it had been to let the dead girl know they'd caught her killer.

And here I am again...

As she picked through the Latin, recognizing certain phrases, she realized that Fayne's summoning wasn't specific to one person. It was a general cattle call: If you were buried nearby, come join the party.

What are you doing?

The earth to Riley's right began to groan as if in labor and it soon split apart. A ghostly figure rose from the soil, his tartan in rags. His chiseled face was dirty and smeared with what had to be dried blood and he was armed with a sword in one hand and a dirk in the other.

Riley stared in astonishment. From the style of clothes, this warrior had to have been buried in the mid-seventeen hundreds. Next to him another body rose, then a third. Apparently this had been a battlefield at one time.

A total of nine spectral clansmen heeded the magical call, all armed and ready for war.

"You have no right to do this to them," Riley said, wiggling around in an attempt to get free of the magic that held her in check. "Put them back in their graves!"

"She's right, Fayne. Why are you doing this? The dead shouldn't be disturbed," Brennan insisted.

"They don't care," Fayne replied. "They're only tools, like the two of you."

The summoner was wrong – when the first ghost's eyes met Riley's, the sadness within them nearly made her weep.

Chapter Eleven

Where the hell are they?

Beck shivered involuntarily in the cold night air as he and MacTavish stood outside the manor house. Frantic with worry, he hadn't bothered to grab a coat, and now the wind was playing havoc with the kilt and his thin dress jacket.

"All the cars are still here," Kepler said as he joined them.

Which meant Brennan had taken Riley somewhere on the grounds.

"Up on the hill?" MacTavish asked.

"That would make sense," the other grand master replied.

MacTavish's phone rang. "What'd ya find?" He listened for moment, then ended the call. "I had our housekeeper go up ta the fourth floor and look toward the loch. She says there's a bonfire up there. That's where Fayne will be, and so will the other two."

"How can ya be sure?" Beck said, his gut twisted so hard it was painful to breathe.

"Because it's an old battlefield. Fayne'll be pullin' the dead free from their graves ta keep us busy while she does her spell." At Beck's puzzled expression, he added, "It's what I'd do if I was a spell slinger."

Kepler nodded his agreement. "I'll stay here and keep the manor safe. And I'll put a call into the police. One way or another, they're going to have to be involved."

MacTavish sighed and shook his head in regret. "Aye. Thanks, old friend. Hopefully we can share a wee dram once this hell is over."

Grimly, they set off up the hill, leaving Kepler behind. Beck carried the sword he used in practice sessions, much like the claymore Master Stewart favored though this one wasn't quite as heavy. MacTavish had opted for a similar weapon, but neither of these blades would be of value if the summoner was inside a protective circle.

"Now if she's summoned the dead, the best we can do is keep from gettin' dead ourselves," MacTavish explained. "At least until we break the spell."

"Which means we need to take down the necro," Beck said, pushing forward at a punishing pace.

"Aye," his superior replied. "In case yer wonderin', however that comes ta pass will work for me. Ya ken?"

"Understood. What the hell was Brennan thinkin'?" he demanded.

MacTavish shook his head as they skirted around an outcropping. "I'm not sure. For him ta betray us like that ... in another month or so he'd be workin' directly with Grand Master Alvarez in Mexico. It's an important position and it's taken him nearly a year ta reach that goal."

"Could the necro have put a spell on him?"

"Kepler said he didn't sense one, but Brennan has been a bit odd as of late and I've had ta come down hard on him. I thought it was stress with his final exams comin' up, but now we know different."

Beck thought back through some of the conversations he'd had with Brennan. "Ya know, he said somethin' about envyin' me because I was gonna be a grand master. Didn't make any sense at the time, not after what it took to get here."

MacTavish frowned in through. "Maybe that's it – he's jealous of what we are."

"Yeah," Beck murmured. *If he only knew what bein' a grand master really means.*

As they hiked up the hill, the wind whistling around Beck's knees and the bushes snagging on his kilt, he cursed himself for leaving Riley so vulnerable. He'd promised to keep her safe and failed ... *again.*

"We'll get her back," his superior insisted.

Beck knew when someone was telling you stuff that they didn't necessarily believe.

"Riley will fight her," he said. "She won't give up."

"She'll have ta, because if she gives in she's dead," MacTavish replied. "I'm guessin' that Fayne's people did a test run at the graveyard with that demon. This time she'll go for the real prize."

"A Fallen angel," Beck said, his heart sinking. He'd prayed he'd never have to fight one of those things again, but it just might come to that. *Anything to keep Riley from bein' hurt.* If he failed, and died, would he go to Hell again? Somehow he doubted his mother would show him the way out a second time.

"If she does summon a Fallen, what about the manor? The Archives?" Beck asked. The centuries of knowledge the grand masters had accumulated, often at the cost of their lives.

"Kepler will ensure the wards will hold."

Beck sighed in relief.

Unfortunately those wards weren't going to do a damned thing for either of them.

~ ~ ~ ~ ~

Though her panic continued to discover new thresholds with each passing minute, Riley forced herself to think through the situation. From what she could tell there didn't appear to be too much to work with, at least something that allowed her to walk away from this alive. Allowed her to see Beck again and tell him she loved him, that she trusted him and really wished he'd ask *that* question one more time.

Riley turned her attention to the words written on the piece of paper in front of her, in the hope that they might be of assistance. When she reached out to pick up the paper, sharp magic nipped at her fingers like a hungry bird, forcing her hand back. Leaning closer, she tried to read the script, but the words blurred. Another one of Fayne's tricks.

Riley guessed that once her blood touched that paper, the spell would direct dial one of Lucifer's top menaces. If Fayne could bind it to her will, there was no way the necromancer was going to allow Brennan to kill it. If she didn't, Fayne was inside a protective circle. No harm, no foul, at least from the summoner's point of view.

As Riley's despair deepened, a familiar warmth brushed her mind, her father's spirit, who was never that far away, even on good days. She recalled his mussed brown hair, how he always had a kiss and a hug for her. How much he had loved her mother.

You're stronger than you know, Paul Blackthorne whispered in that firm, yet loving tone he used to ensure she was listening.

How do I stop her?

Be yourself. Be stronger than she is.

The utter suckage of the situation made Riley's anger burn. Who the hell was this woman anyway? *If I could just get free...* She wiggled again, like a toddler stuck in a highchair, and just as helpless. Around her, the dead warriors fanned out.

"Riley!" Beck called out as he and MacTavish came out of the darkness. Just as he began hurrying toward her, the grand master made a futile grab at his arm.

"Careful, lad," MacTavish called out.

His warning came quick enough for Beck to evade one of the ghosts, who had surged forward, swinging its sword. The instant he backed off, the specter ceased its attack.

"If you remain in place, they won't hurt you," Fayne said, magic encircling her like a swarm of bees.

Beck ignored her. "Damn you, Brennan! What the hell are ya doin'?"

"Don't worry, she'll be safe," Brennan said, but Riley could see sweat glistening on his face now.

"That's a load and ya know it," MacTavish replied, his voice dripping with acid. "Why have ya done this, lad? Why have ya betrayed one of our own?"

"To prove I'm as good as any of you," the young man retorted. "Fayne will summon a Fallen and when I kill it, then I'll be one of you. You'll have to let me in, that's the rules."

"She's been feedin' ya this nonsense, hasn't she?" MacTavish said, angling his head toward the necromancer.

"Of course I have," Fayne said, without a hint of remorse. "He wants to be a grand master, I want to summon a Fallen. That's synergy."

"It'll work, you'll see," Brennan said.

"No, it won't. And God help ya, yer about to learn a very hard lesson, ya damned fool."

Before Brennan could reply, the compulsion spell hit Riley like an arrow embedding itself deep in her forehead. On their own volition, her fingers reached out to grasp the knife, slowly turning the silver blade toward her. She tried to let go of the weapon, turn it away, but Fayne's spell was too strong.

No, not like this.

"Riley, what are ya doin?" Beck called.

"It's not me. It's her. She's making me do it."

"Ah, hell!"

He hacked at one of the ghosts, cutting it in half, but it promptly reassembled, preventing him from reaching her.

"Fayne?" MacTavish growled. "There'll be no goin' back if the girl dies. Ya ken?"

The necromancer laughed, cold and sharp. "She is of no importance. If I command a Fallen, you can do nothing."

Realization dawned in Brennan's eyes. He whirled toward the necromancer. "You told me she wouldn't be hurt!"

Fayne shrugged. "I might have lied about that."

"You bitch! I don't want this if she's going to be hurt."

"You have no choice now."

Brennan swore and strode closer, ready to do battle, but found himself pushed away by a pair of the ghosts.

Riley's eyes were riveted on the blade now, her hands burning at the effort to keep it away from her. Even as she fought it, it slipped closer. If she gave in to the spell, it would be one hard thrust, a quick death.

"Let it go, child," Fayne urged. "Don't fight it. You know you want to. For once in your life you'll have peace."

Peace? No way.

Despite the spell, Riley's mind delivered a clear image of the blade slashing into her neck, slicing across, severing the arteries. Her life blood pumping onto the ground while Beck watched her die in helpless fury.

"Quick or slow, it doesn't matter to me," Fayne said, her hands glowing like sparkling fireflies. "It will happen either way."

"Riley, please. Don't let her do this to ya," Beck called out. He'd shifted to a position where she could see him out of the corner of her eye. As long as he didn't move any closer, the nearest ghosts held their position. She could see the agony on his face, the realization that he had no way to prevent her death.

"I can't..." Riley said, tears rolling down her cheeks. "She's too strong."

The moment the words were out, the knife shot closer, within inches of her throat.

"Weakness will kill ya," MacTavish called out. "Be stronger than her."

"I—"

"Ya were stronger than Hell. Ya outwitted Lucifer himself. *This* is only a damned necromancer, a pale imitation of that evil. Fight her!" MacTavish roared.

You can do this, her father's voice said. *You have too much to live for.*

Tears were on Beck's face now, coursing down his reddened cheeks, his body quaking. "Riley, I love ya. I need ya, girl. Don't let her kill us both."

The blade slid closer again, pausing only an inch from her skin. She swore she could feel her blood being lured toward the sharp edge as the   spell kept urging her to give in, to accept her fate.

If you do, Beck and the others are dead, her father warned. *She will leave no witnesses.*

Her eyes sought Beck's. *I love you.*

"Riley," he said, his voice hoarse. "Please..."

She locked onto his face, feeling the end was near. The muscles in her arms and neck were burning in agony now, her heart beating so fast she could barely catch her breath. Shadows began to form at the edges of her vision, the beginnings of a panic attack.

"Riley? Ya see that ring on yer right hand? My grandmamma's ring? That's our future, girl. That's us together, havin' our own home. Maybe, when yer older, someday havin' kids." He sucked in a deep breath. "We lose it all if ya let this bitch win."

Fayne issued a throaty laugh. "You really can't believe that will work, do you?"

Beck's anger exploded and he took a few steps forward. "Nothin' is worth her life. Use my blood, dammit. Hell wants a piece of me."

"Or what, little grand master? You have no power here. Once I command a Fallen angel, I can do whatever I want."

With a roar, Beck charged the closest ghost, hacking at it with his sword. Brennan engaged another one of the dead clansman, slicing at him, trying to break through. MacTavish joined them, but they were badly outnumbered.

In an instant, Beck was down, dazed by a blow. As he tried to regain his feet, Brennan stepped in front of him, holding the specter back. The ghost's blade caught him high on the shoulder and he shrieked in pain and fell. Beck came to his feet, his fierce blows raining down the ghost, pushing it back to allow Brennan cover.

Riley felt the compulsion spell weaken as Fayne's concentration lessened.

Now! her father called out.

Perspiration beading on her forehead, Riley gritted her teeth and pulled back on the blade. To her surprise, it retreated by an inch or so. Fortunately, Fayne didn't notice, too busy savoring the battle.

A little more. I can do this. I will do this.

Sweating like it was mid-summer in Atlanta, her hands throbbing as if she was holding molten metal, Riley yanked the blade away from her throat. On instinct, she rammed the knife hilt deep into Scottish soil, grounding the magic before Fayne could react.

To Riley's astonishment, the compulsion spell blew apart, the power released rolling across the open ground like a magical tsunami. It cracked against the protective circle and shattered it like fragile glass. Fayne shrieked as she rocketed backward in the air and landed in a tangled heap.

There were shouts from both Beck and MacTavish as the magic struck them as well. Then silence fell. Riley's heart continued to pound and she forced herself to take one slow breath after another.

When she finally opened her eyes, her hands were still knotted around the handle of the blade, but none of her blood had been spilt.

Well done, her father murmured. *I knew you could do it.*

"Thanks, Dad," she murmured.

Riley slowly raised her head. A quick glance proved that Beck and MacTavish were unhurt and slowly rising to their feet. Unnervingly, the nine warriors were ranged in a semi-circle around her now, all down on one knee, their heads bowed.

"What have you done?" Fayne cried. Magic burst from her fingers, but fizzled away. "They are mine!" she said and tried again, as her nose bleeding.

The deep voice of the lead warrior broke the night, thick with an old Scottish brogue which should have been barely recognizable to Riley's modern mind. Still she understood his words.

"What would ya have us do, mistress?" he asked.

"I would..." Riley swallowed to a dry throat. "I would have you ... go to your graves and rest in peace, never to rise again."

The man inclined his head, and when he straightened up she saw gratitude in his eyes. "As ya command, mistress."

One by one, the ghosts silently filed back to their individual graves and sank deep into the ground, sealing them into the earth like the day they'd been buried centuries before.

Fayne was moaning now, blood streaming from her nose, the spell's rebound having taken its toll.

Riley blinked her eyes, trying to clear her vision, but it didn't work. Through the fog she could see Beck and MacTavish regain their feet. Neither of them appeared hurt, though Brennan was, his side covered in blood.

She held her hands out in front of her, watching the purple energy dance across her fingers.

That's so cool. It reminded her of how her body had glowed after the cemetery battle in Atlanta, after she'd stood her ground between the forces of Heaven and Hell.

She placed her palms flat on the ground and let the magic course out of her. As it flowed away, like a river, her vision cleared. When it was done, she flopped on her back, staring up at the stars like when she was a kid. The night was clearer now, fewer clouds, and she swore she could see infinity.

"Now ya can go ta her," MacTavish said.

Beck pounded across the open space and then fell at her side, heedless of the stones that dug into his bare knees.

"Riley?" he asked, peering down at her, a smear of blood on his cheek.

She pointed upward like a small child would, a faint remnant of magic playing along her knuckles. "The stars. They're so big here. Too much light at home. Never see them that well."

"Riley?" he said, again, more urgently now. "Are ya okay?"

A meteor shot across the black sky and she made a wish. If she was lucky, it just might come true. When it faded from view she looked over at Beck. "Wow. We're still alive. How about that?" she said.

A grin slowly formed on his handsome face. "Yer awesome, girl. And yer mine. Always will be. And I will rain Hell on anyone who thinks different."

Then my wish has already come true.

Chapter Twelve

After giving Riley his jacket, Beck had no choice but to help Brennan, whose shoulder wound was bleeding heavily. While MacTavish kept a stern eye on the necromancer, Beck stripped off his waistcoat and shirt. The wind immediately bit at him, making him shiver. He slipped back on the waistcoat, though it was next to useless in terms of warmth.

"This is gonna hurt," Beck said, then pressed the shirt into Brennan's shoulder wound to slow the bleeding. His anger found its focus. "Ya know, I should let you bleed out for what you did to Riley."

Brennan moaned in response, his face ashen. "I never meant ... to hurt her."

"The hell ya didn't. Ya ... you knew Fayne was batshit crazy."

"I thought..." Brennan shook his head. "Wanted to be ... like you," he continued, his voice fainter now. "A grand master."

"Why?"

"I just wanted ... to matter. You know? Not be a loser."

Beck reared back, wincing as a flash of memory hit close to home. Ever since he was a kid, he'd wanted the same thing, to matter in this life. Not to be a total loser. Only fate, and Riley's love, had given him that chance.

Oh, shit...

He and Brennan's eyes met. He could continue to hate on this guy or ... understand him. Beck cleared his throat. "I kinda know how that goes. You just took it too far."

"I know," Brennan whispered. "Tell her I'm sorry. Please?"

"You can tell her yerself. Just hang in there."

"No, you'll have to tell her. I betrayed the grand masters. I'm a dead man. You know it too."

Beck grimaced. "We'll see," was the best he could offer.

Riley's head spun, then righted as she kept taking deep breaths. She watched as a trio of police officers hurried across the crown of the hill, as well as emergency personnel. She guessed that Kepler had summoned them. Given Brennan's injury, it was a wise move.

MacTavish gave the officers a quick summary of the night's drama, but to Riley's surprise he wasn't completely forthcoming. Somehow he didn't mention that Brennan had been armed when he'd kidnapped Riley, only that the man had forced her to come to the necromancer. That once he had been treated, he was to be returned to the grand masters. But how would they handle Brennan's crimes? She feared the answer.

Once the wounded man was being treated by the paramedics, Beck returned to her side, his hands bloody. He looked exhausted.

"How's Brennan?" she asked.

"Hurt pretty bad." Another round of shivering ensued, though he tried to suppress it.

Riley pulled off his jacket and offered it to him.

"No, I'm good. Besides, I thought you liked it when I don't wear a shirt."

She groaned, once again amazed how guys could be so weird. "I do like you without a shirt – when it's not twenty below zero."

"You need it more than I do."

Riley shoved the jacket into his hands and watched him work through his conflicting emotions. "Just take it, okay? Stop being so stubborn."

He blinked at her, then apparently realized now was not the time to challenge her. "Thanks." He slipped on the jacket.

She looked toward paramedics and their patient. "Brennan saved your life."

"Yeah," Beck replied, clearly uncomfortable. "I'm not sure if that is going to help him much in the long run."

Riley rose on her own, though he tried to help her. She glanced toward the necromancer, and, without a word of warning to Beck, headed that direction before he could protest. He fell in step next to her, his arm around her waist for support.

Riley halted at the edge of the now defunct circle, her body still tingling from the magic. Her enemy stared up at her, Fayne's chin and chest covered in drying blood. MacTavish stood nearby.

"You blew my compulsion spell apart like it was nothing," Fayne rasped. "No trapper could have done that. What the hell are you?"

Riley chose to ignore the question, mostly because she had no answer.

"Remove the spell from Bess' daughter," she ordered.

"Why should I?"

MacTavish lined up his sword under the necromancer's throat. "Because if ya don't, ya die right here. One way or another, that spell is gone, ya ken?"

"Sir?" one of the cops said, taking a cautious step forward. "I don't think that's a good idea."

"This is grand master business, lad, not yers," MacTavish warned, his tone as sharp as his steel. "Best not ta get involved."

One of the other officers whispered something to the first one and they stepped back, clearly nervous. That told Riley everything she needed to know about how much power the grand masters wielded.

"So what will it be, Fayne?" MacTavish asked, his sword never wavering.

After a furious glare at him, the necromancer gave a sharp nod. "Once I've rested, I'll reverse the spell."

The journey down the hill felt surreal. Riley was warmer now, wrapped in a blanket, courtesy of one of the cops. Beck walked beside her with sure footsteps, the kilt swaying with each step, his sword resting on his right shoulder like a warrior from another century.

You belong here. This is your home as much as it is Stewart's.

He caught her looking at him. "I screwed up everything. I'm sorry I didn't keep ya safe," he began, his voice quavering. "I should have seen this comin'."

She could argue that no one had, not even MacTavish, but Beck would never listen. He was all about protecting her, just as she was about him.

That's our greatest strength ... and our greatest weakness.

As she made her way toward the manor house, Riley had the profound sense that her life had changed, again. She wasn't sure how she felt about that.

"What will they do with Fayne?" she asked.

"Something damned permanent, I hope," Beck replied. "If not, I'll make sure she doesn't pull this kind of shit again."

Something Stewart said came back to her, how some parts of his job as a grand master were very painful.

"What happens if one of you guys goes dark, starts working with Hell?"

Beck took a quick intake of breath as if she'd struck a nerve. "That person dies." He hesitated, then added, "Same thing if it's a master trapper."

His tone chilled her. "You mean Stewart would have had to kill my dad if he'd really been working for Hell?"

"Yes," Beck said solemnly. "It's no comfort, but Paul would have wanted it that way."

The full reality of what he'd said rolled out in front of her.

"You'd have to do that, I mean if... ?"

"It's how it works. It's how we keep the balance between good and evil."

And if I went dark?

Beck looked over at her, as if he'd heard her. "If you become a master demon trapper and you ... start workin' for Hell, one of us will come for you."

Riley stumbled to a halt. "And you'd let them do that?" she asked, fearing the answer.

"No. I'd do everythin' I could to protect you. I would never let them hurt you."

"But that would put you against your own people. Make you just as bad as I would be."

His eyes met hers and she saw the raw pain in them now. "If that's what it takes."

My God...

She took hold of his chilly hand. "No. If I ever go dark ... let them do what they have to do."

He looked away, unable to speak.

"Don't worry, I'll make sure I never go there."

"Sometimes that's a hard promise to keep. You know how Hell works."

"I know, but I won't do anything that puts your life on the line."

Because she knew if he tried to save her, his people would kill them both.

Nothing Hell has to offer is worth that sacrifice.

There'd been no more conversation until they'd reached their room, and in some ways, Beck was good with that. He'd been meaning to tell her more about a grand master's duties, but she'd already worked it out in her head.

Now she knows. At least that part. There was more, a lot more, but now was not the time.

~ - ~ - ~

Riley had insisted she didn't want a shower, even when he offered to help her. Instead, she chucked off her outer clothes and he tucked her in bed. As it was so often in their past, they were just going through the motions, trying to act like nothing horrible had happened.

She had scared the living hell out of him tonight. Seeing that blade pointed at her throat had driven home how much he loved her, how much he had to lose if she wasn't by his side. Even now, Beck wanted to shake her, insist that she couldn't run from her magical abilities any longer, not when she'd just blown a spell back on a mid-level summoner. Once word of that got out it'd play one of two ways: most folks would respect her and back off. Others would take it as a challenge and come after Riley, just to up their mojo.

Now, curled up in bed, she seemed so frail, so vulnerable.

"I love you," she said simply.

"Right back at you," he whispered.

Riley closed her eyes and fell into an uneasy sleep.

Beck sat with her for a time, watching each gentle breath, his emotions as sharp as acid dripping onto his flesh. Most of it was anger and fear at how close he'd come to losing her.

Would the night's horrors bring them closer together, or would she back off, not want anything to do with him now that she knew what he faced as a grand master? He shook his head, not wanting to consider a future without her.

After a trip to the bathroom to wash off Brennan's blood, he pulled on a pair of jeans and a heavy sweatshirt, relishing the warmth. He placed a kiss on Riley's forehead, then quietly left the room.

He found MacTavish and Kepler talking in the front hallway, the cops gone and the house quiet. As Beck approached, they turned toward him.

"How's she doin'?" MacTavish asked.

"She's asleep. Totally worn out."

"She threw off a strong spell, she'll probably sleep for some time," Kepler advised.

"What about Brennan?"

"He's in hospital. They think they can save his arm," Kepler replied

"Thank God. He said he did it just because he wanted to be like us," Beck said. *Like me.*

"His damned foolishness cost three lives," MacTavish grumbled.

"If Fayne hadn't talked him into helpin' her, she would have found someone else. Someone with less of a conscience." Beck paused, marshaling his thoughts. "Sometimes it's so important to matter in this world that you do dumb stuff, things you'd never do otherwise."

The grand masters traded looks.

"Aye," MacTavish replied, his voice quieter now. "But accordin' ta our laws, he should already have been put ta the sword for betrayin' us."

"He saved my life," Beck said. "That should count for somethin', don't you think?"

"Maybe," MacTavish admitted. "We'll have ta think on it."

"I'd like to be in on any decision you make. It's personal now."

A pause, then a nod. "As ya wish."

Beck knew that was as far as he could push the matter. "What about that necro? Is she gonna stay put in jail?"

"Aye, she will. I've called her superiors," MacTavish replied. "I let them know that either they deal with her, or we do. One way or the other, she is out of the magic business *forever.*"

"Works for me," Beck allowed. "Thanks, both of you. You kept Riley alive, and I owe you."

"Glad we could help out," Kepler replied. "She should be fine from now on."

"God, I hope so." With a respectful nod at both grand masters, Beck turned on a heel and headed back to the room, to be by her side.

Even if she doesn't want me anymore.

Riley woke wrapped in a strong and comforting embrace. *Den.* It reminded her of being back in Atlanta, how sometimes she'd stay overnight at his place and then wake in the morning, knowing how much he loved her.

As she took inventory she was relieved to find that her body no longer tingled. In fact, she felt stronger, more clear headed, like she'd been before she'd come to Scotland.

About time.

The clock indicated it was somewhere near five, and the birds roosting in the trees agreed, chirping to announce the new day.

As she listened to Beck's even breaths, Riley knew she had a choice: She could step away from him now, let him go his own way, or they could move forward, try to mend what had been broken.

Either way, he would expect her to make the first move.

When she slipped out of his arms, he woke immediately. "You

okay?" he asked groggily.

"I'm good. I need a shower."

"I'll be here when yer done," he murmured and curled back into a sleepy ball.

Smiling to herself at the sight, Riley closed the door to the bathroom. As she stripped out of her underwear, her nose crinkled in disgust: all she could smell was dirt, smoke and cast-off magic. Somehow Beck hadn't noticed all that, or at least had been too polite to mention it.

Later, when she exited the bathroom, he was awake again, his head propped up on a palm. A lazy Southern smile welcomed her, along with those deep brown eyes.

"Hey there, Princess," he said, his attention drifting to the extra large bath towel she wore. The smile was all bad boy, at least for a few seconds, then he sobered. "Ah ... Where are we? I mean ... are we good again, like it used to be ... or..."

Riley halted, uneasy. "Do you want it to be that way? Like before?"

Beck sat up now, tucking the sheet around his hips. His worried expression telegraphed he was as terrified of this moment as she was.

He took a deep breath.

Oh God, he's going to back away. He can't handle all this.

"Yes, I want us to be together. I don't give a damn about anythin' else."

"Even being a grand master?" she asked, though that really wasn't a fair question.

To her surprise, the nod came instantly. "I know this is important work, but I'd give it up if you asked me to. You are my life, Riley."

Wow.

But that wouldn't be right. "No, you're supposed to be a grand master, or you wouldn't have killed Sartael, made it out of Hell. That was your destiny."

He sighed. "Yeah, I guess. But me bein' a grand master will cause problems between us, you have to know that."

"I do. And what I do causes problems too. That's us, I guess."

"So then," Beck paused to clear his throat. "Are you comin' back to this bed as a friend ... or as my girl?" he asked, his voice husky.

Riley unhooked the bath towel and it fell away.

The bad boy smile was back. He grinned at the sight of her, bruises and all. "I'd say that answers my question."

Riley slid in next to him, tentatively touching his face, feeling the beard stubble as she pulled him down for a kiss. His body pressed against her, warm, strong and alive.

The way forward was clear, no doubts, no insecurity for either of them. There were few words after that, only the unspoken promise that no matter what the world threw at them, they were still one, and always would be.

Chapter Thirteen

It was late in the morning when Riley finally roused. There hadn't been much sleep, not with Beck eager to "welcome her to Scotland" more than once. There was no way she regretted the lost sleep. It was like she'd dreamed – the two of them together, loving.

Beck was in her shower, singing one of Carrie Underwood's songs with that resonant voice of his. He sounded truly happy, and it filled her heart with so much joy she thought it would burst. This is what she wanted to hear every morning for the rest of her life. But would he be brave enough to ask her that question again?

She frowned. *If he doesn't, I'll ask him. One way or another, we're together.*

The shower shut off and a short time later Beck appeared in the doorway, towel around his waist and his damp hair hanging loosely on his shoulders. With his sculpted muscles and drop-dead looks, he never failed to make her heart double beat.

"Hey you," she said, sitting up, pulling the sheet up with her.

"Good mornin'," he said, sitting next her. A kiss came next, tasting of minty toothpaste. Then Beck handed over his phone. "Sorry, but duty calls. Seems I got a text while I was showerin'. Guess MacTavish didn't want to interrupt us or anythin'."

SNR NECROS HERE @ 1. WANT TO MEET W/RILEY

She sighed. "Oh, crap."

"If you don't want to talk to them, just say so. MacTavish will understand," Beck said, watching her closely. "Though I bet this'll be more an interrogation than a talk, if you know what I mean."

She did, but for some reason she wasn't afraid of these guys.

Not anymore.

"Yes, I want to chat with these people," she said, a crooked smile edging in place. "In fact, I'm looking forward to it."

Beck caught her tone and executed a whistle. "Ya've got that 'I'm gonna kick some ass' look. These guys are in trouble, aren't they?"

Riley grinned. "Damned straight," she said.

MacTavish had arranged for the meeting to be held in the room with the overstuffed chairs, the cozy fireplace and the cabinet well stocked with liquor. Riley was more interested in the contents of the elegant silver teapot. Somehow she'd become seriously addicted to Scottish Breakfast tea and she hoped that Stewart could find a supply for her back in Atlanta, or the withdrawal symptoms were going to be ugly.

With a steaming cup in hand, she chose a chair near Beck. He smiled over at her, touching her hand fondly where it sat on the armrest.

"This is yer show," he said. "I'm just here to make sure no one tries to hurt you."

Riley nodded back, nervous, but not panicking like she had before her interrogation by the Vatican's Demon Hunters. She hadn't told Beck, but there was something new in her blood now and it had begun the moment the knife had plunged deep into Scottish soil. Maybe it had something to do with the old magic in this place, or maybe it was the fierce pride of the Scots. The English had their own pride as well, and now it coursed through her veins like strong wine, making her keen to settle scores. Determined to ensure that her future was her own, not destroyed at the whim of others.

Riley finished the tea and set the cup aside just as MacTavish entered the room. He gave them both a nod, then chose the chair nearest the fire.

"How are the pair of ya this mornin?" he asked, a twinkle in his eyes.

"Fine. Right fine," Beck replied.

"Truly?"

"Yup," Riley said. "It's all good."

"Thank God," MacTavish replied.

"How much do these necros know about what happened last night?" Riley asked.

"I told the summoners pretty much everythin', except I might have forgotten ta mention that Fayne was tryin' ta summon a Fallen angel."

"Did she tell them?"

He shook his head. "Fayne refuses to talk to them. Maybe ya'd like ta drop that little bomb on them yerself."

Riley grinned in anticipation. "I'll do just that."

With a deep inhalation, she steeled herself as the door opened and Kepler joined them. He was followed by two summoners, one of each gender. The woman was about a decade younger than Kepler, with silver hair in a tidy bun, her robe deepest black which denoted her as a powerful necromancer. The man was probably in his fifties given the silver at his temples. His robe was darkest brown, which told Riley his skills were at Mort level or just below.

The visitors took chairs next to each other, their movements wary.

"This is Summoner Marian Enfield," Kepler said as he indicated the woman, "and Summoner Thomas Minton," as he shifted his hand toward the man. "They are the most senior necromancers in the United Kingdom. They wish to discuss what happened overnight."

"Surprise," Riley murmured.

"We are here, Miss Blackthorne," Ms. Enfield began with a polished English accent, "to ascertain precisely what occurred between you and Summoner Fayne over the past week."

"So ask your questions."

Enfield shifted in her chair. "What is your relationship to Summoner Fayne?"

"None, other than the fact she tried to kill me, *twice,*" Riley replied.

"Certainly there had to be some involvement," the woman countered. "Why else would she include you in her activities?

What pact did you make between you?"

Pact?

Riley leaned back in her chair, consciously relaxing her posture. If she acted as if she was spooked, that would give them the upper hand.

"There was no pact. I'd never met the woman before."

"Still–"

"Do you usually let newbie necromancers loose with demonic summoning spells?" Riley asked. "Because Robbie certainly wasn't skilled enough to try that kind of incantation. He couldn't even create a solid ward."

Enfield frowned. "No, we don't allow our newer members to do such things."

"Is that just a no-no for the newbies, or how about the rest of you? I'd think you'd not want anyone messing around with the demons."

"None of this sort of behavior happened until you arrived in Scotland, Miss Blackthorne." A tiny muscle at the corner of the woman's right eye twitched. It was so slight, Riley might have missed it if she hadn't been looking for it.

You're lying.

"I bet Fayne's done this kind of thing before. So where'd she get the spell?" Riley asked.

"Perhaps you gave it to her," Minton replied, jumping into the conversation.

Beck tensed. "Why would you think that?"

"What other conclusion may we draw?" Minton continued. He adjusted his robe thoughtfully. "Why else would one of our summoners attempt an *advanced* spell the moment this child arrives in Edinburgh?"

The "child" part rankled, but Riley let it pass. "Why would I want one of you guys to summon a demon for me? It's not like we're running low on them here or back home. What would be the point?"

"Is it not true that a trapper must slay an Archfiend before your National Guild allows you to become a master?" Ms. Enfield asked.

"Perhaps that opportunity has eluded you in the past and you saw a way to rectify that problem."

Beck huffed in disgust. "Riley killed an Archfiend last spring. She's already met that requirement."

Enfield hesitated for a moment – clearly she hadn't known that bit of news. "And yet, she is not a Master Demon Trapper. How can that be?"

"Indeed, perhaps she felt that slaying another demon might hasten the process," Minton added.

They were talking around her now. Curiously, the two grand masters were staying out this, watching it play out like a complex chess game.

"No, you're wrong. Taking down another Archfiend will only made it harder for me," Riley said. "The National Guild will think I did it to make them look like idiots."

Which wasn't that hard.

"So you claim," Minton retorted.

"That's the way it is," she replied. "You're just going to have to deal."

"Your lack of respect is troubling," Ms. Enfield replied, bristling.

Riley glanced at MacTavish again. No comment; he must have been good with how she was handling this so she pressed on.

"Respect goes both ways," she said. "You screwed up and now you're trying to drop this whole mess on *my* head. That's not going to fly."

"Aye, the lass is right," MacTavish cut in. "It is *yer* responsibility ta keep yer people honest. Ya've been doin' a damned poor job of it lately."

Summoner Enfield glowered at him. "What we do is our own business, *Grand Master.* It's not like your kind are all on the straight and narrow."

MacTavish issued a solemn nod. "And those grand masters who strayed off the path are now in their graves. Can the same be said of yours?"

"We are not so barbaric," was the acidic reply.

This pissing match wasn't getting at the truth.

"You knew Fayne had the spell," Riley began, "and you let her run with it. If she'd failed to summon a demon, no big deal. If she did, you'd know the spell worked and your hands wouldn't have blood on them. You didn't plan on her using someone else to do a test run, or that those folks would end up dead."

Minton winced, which was as much of an admission of guilt as Riley would ever receive.

"Is that what happened?" Beck asked.

Enfield ignored him which only pushed Riley's buttons. Beck deserved respect – he was a master trapper in his own right.

"*Master* Beck asked you a question. You should answer it. His life was on the line last night, just as much as mine was."

The senior necromancer huffed. "After the unfortunate incident at the graveyard, we spoke to Fayne, told her back off," Ms. Enfield admitted. "She promised she would. In fact, she offered to apologize to you, which is why she was here at the dinner last evening instead of us, as originally planned."

"She certainly didn't apologize," Kepler said quietly.

"No, she was here to make sure I came to her little summoning party. You see, I wasn't using the Holy Water she'd bespelled, so she had to be here in person to ensure Brennan got me up the hill."

"It was a simple mistrust spell," Kepler explained. "It makes the victim paranoid, distrustful. Prone to irrational decisions."

Beck touched Riley's hand and then clutched it, hard.

"Except my wounds healed too fast and I stopped using it." Riley gently pulled her hand loose and moved to the fireplace, buying time as she thought through her next move. Kneeling, she picked up the poker and jabbed at a log, moving it back in place so the flames could consume it.

By the time she rose, she was ready. "Last night's spell was different," she said. "Fayne wasn't summoning a demon."

"Then what were you summoning?" Minton asked.

That pissed her off. "*I* wasn't summoning anything. I was the one with the knife at my throat."

"What is your point?" Ms. Enfield demanded. "Or is this all histrionics?"

Riley swung toward her. "My point? Last spring, in Atlanta, one of our necromancers decided to summon a demon. He got a Fallen angel instead, one named Sartael, who was really keen to take Lucifer's throne. When it was all over, a lot of people died and we came *very* close to Armageddon."

"Surely you are exaggerating," Enfield replied.

"She's not," Beck replied. "Went down just like she said."

"But what has that to do with us?" Minton asked, frowning now.

Riley returned to her chair. "What do you know about Lord Ozymandias?" she asked, hoping they weren't aware that he was the one who had summoned Sartael.

The summoners traded looks.

"His lordship is well regarded, a very powerful summoner," the woman replied. "Some say one of the most powerful in America."

"And compared to you?"

Ms. Enfield's eyes narrowed. "His lordship is infinitely more skilled than I am. I hope one day to attain that level of magical competency." She frowned. "But what does this have to do with this situation?"

"Lord Ozymandias was the necromancer who tried to summon a demon and got a Fallen angel instead. For all his power, Ozy became Sartael's bitch. That's how much power those things have. It took a major battle and..." She looked over at Beck, "a few brave people before Sartael was defeated and Ozy was freed."

Enfield gave MacTavish a dubious look, but he just nodded. She swallowed heavily. "Then, I'll accept that this may ... have happened as you said, but what has this to do with Fayne? Surely you can't be saying that she was going to summon an angel."

"That's exactly what I'm saying. Last night's spell required a blood sacrifice. *My blood.* Because your necromancer was calling up a Fallen."

The two summoners' faces paled at exactly the same instant.

"No, not possible. Fayne doesn't have kind the power," Minton insisted.

"She was conducting the spell inside what used to be an old

stone circle, a magical locus," Kepler said. "If Fayne had succeeded in forcing Riley to cut her own throat, a Fallen angel *would* have appeared."

"But surely –" Minton began, looking over at MacTavish now, "you would have been able to kill it."

"There would have been no guarantee," the grand master admitted. "If we hadn't, the thing would have been free ta rain destruction throughout the country. Guess who would have been blamed for that?"

Enfield traded a horrified look with her companion.

Riley crossed her arms over her chest. It was time to lay out the terms.

"Here's how it's going to work: I will not go to the newspapers and tell them exactly what happened on that hill last night, or what happened at the graveyard. I won't tell your countrymen that one of *your people* almost brought Hell to their doorsteps. If the reporters find out on their own, that's your problem, not mine. If I'm called into court to testify, same thing."

"But–" Enfield began.

Riley held up her hand for silence. "In exchange for my silence you will make sure that Fayne's spell on Bess' daughter is really gone. You will make sure that she *never* does magic again. And you will get Bess an attorney, and pay all her legal costs, because it was *your* summoner who blackmailed her into that graveyard in the first place."

"We–"

"I'm not done." Riley pushed on. "You will ride herd on your people, and if one of them is working demonic magic, they will pay the price."

"Umm ... certainly we will talk to that person, and convince them to–" Minton began.

"No!" Riley said, slamming her hands down on the arms of the chair. "That's not good enough! Do you know what Ozymandias does when one of his people summons a demon? He kills them. They're just little bits of ash in the wind. There are *no* second chances, because he knows exactly how many innocent people can die when one of you guys gets stupid."

Enfield's mouth dropped open. "Surely you're jesting. His lordship would never—"

"She's not lyin'," Beck said, his tone brittle. "Ozymandias learned the hard way, and he's damned if anyone else is gonna make the same effin' mistake."

"We ... shall have to take this under advisement," Enfield said.

Riley remembered Callan and the others, the terror of their last few minutes alive. Furious at the summoners' stalling, pulled her cell phone out of her jeans pocket.

"How about I call Ozy and let him know what's up over here? See what he thinks? It's not a problem. He's on speed dial." Which was a total lie. But Mort was, and he was only one phone call away from the high lord himself.

At her outrageous offer, Enfield reared back in astonishment, panic in her eyes now. Clearly she hadn't thought Riley was *that* plugged in.

"Ah ... no. That won't be necessary," the woman sputtered. "We wouldn't want to ... inconvenience his lordship."

You guys are so full of it.

"As I see it," Beck began in that deceptively lazy drawl of his, "it depends on whether y'all have the balls to police yer own, or if yer just in this for the fancy robes."

Minton actually snarled, but his superior put her hand on his arm.

"We're done here," she said.

In more ways than one.

The summoners had just reached the door before Enfield turned back toward her, expression grave.

"How did you reverse Fayne's spell? Did Lord Ozymandias teach you how to do that?"

Riley shook her head. "I'm just a Journeyman Demon Trapper."

"No trapper can do what you did last night," the summoner shot back. "What the hell *are* you, girl?"

Curiously, Fayne had asked the same question. This time, Riley knew the answer. She rose and took a step closer to the pair, and was pleased to see them tense in response.

"*What* am I? I'm Paul Blackthorne's daughter."

"You're more than that."

Riley nodded in agreement. "You're right. I'm also the girl who bargained with the Archangel Michael and prevented the end of the world. With the help of a friend, I even outsmarted Lucifer and got my soul back. I've been to Hell and hope to see Heaven. And even the demons know my name." Riley raised an eyebrow, pitching her voice just right. "Now you do, too. Remember that, if you *ever* come after me or mine again."

Enfield blinked and shot an astounded glance toward MacTavish, as if seeking confirmation of Riley's outrageous claims.

"It's the absolute truth," he replied. "And her threat wasn't an idle one, either. Best ya heed it."

"My God," Minton murmured, his face pale once again.

The tension held for a few seconds, vibrating in the air like right before a lightning strike, then the summoners swept out the door, stunned into submission.

"I'll make sure they don't lose their way," Kepler said, following after them. Riley swore she heard him chuckling.

The moment the door shut behind them, Beck grabbed onto her and swung her around, awe stamped on his face. "Damn, Riley girl, that was kick ass."

It had been. And though it had felt good to unload like that, she knew her warning was probably wasted effort. "They won't listen," she said, staring at the closed door as he'd set her down. "They think they're too smart to get trapped. Just like Ozy."

MacTavish nodded in agreement. "I'll make sure ta keep the pressure on them."

"Good luck with that," she replied.

"Ya ken I have to ask; how *did* ya reverse that spell?"

Riley spread her arms, grinning. "I have no freakin' clue."

"Really? And Lord Ozymandias' phone number? Is he really on speed dial?"

"Nope, I might have lied about that."

MacTavish's hearty laughter filled the small room.

Chapter Fourteen

It was later in the afternoon, after another long stressed-induced snooze, that Riley awoke, groggy. Sometime during the nap Beck had crawled in next to her and was asleep, just as worn out as she was. Fighting off evil necromancers had that effect.

Riley padded to the bathroom and on the way back, she halted in front of the window. Then she smiled. Dropping on the bed, she nudged Beck.

"Hey, you," she said, "wake up."

"Hmmm," he said, turning on his back. "What's wrong?"

"It's snowing," she said.

His response was an unintelligible mumble.

"Come, get up, you lazy thing. We have to go outside."

"Why?" he replied, slowly levering open his eyes. "It'll be way cold out there."

"Because it's snowing!"

Not waiting to see if he'd join her, Riley quickly pulled on various layers, then laced up her boots. Beck was still in bed as she closed the door behind her.

Your loss.

Riley stepped outside the front door, inhaling the crisp scent of fresh snow. The cars were covered, as were the bushes that lined the long drive. The dragon statues on either side of the main entrance were coated in the fluffy white stuff, making them appear less fearsome.

Scotland crowned in snow. Riley memorized the moment.

The tap of the snowflakes on her face magically transported her to her childhood when her parents would take her for winter walks when they lived in Chicago. They'd help her make a snowman and snow angels and then they'd have hot chocolate. The innocence of that time came back to her, filling her with a sense of peace that had been missing since the day her mom had died.

The front door opened, then closed as Beck joined her. He was bundled up against the cold, stocking cap in place.

"Let's go up to the loch, okay?" she asked, catching his gloved hand.

"Whatever you want," he said, smiling over at her.

As they climbed the hill, their cloudy breath intermingling, Riley felt they had somehow been transported to another world, just her and Beck together. "It's so quiet."

"Yeah, and damned cold."

"You're such a Georgia boy," she teased.

"Always. Don't have that freeze-proof blood you got bein' born up north."

When they reached the top of the hill, Riley paused, scanning the ground. There was no sign of what had gone down the night before, the grass shrouded in snow, unsullied by magic.

How did I stop Fayne? It was a question that continued to haunt her and would until she talked to Mort.

"You okay?" Beck asked.

"Yeah." She decided not to tell him what was really bothering her, not until she sorted it out in her own head.

They walked on in silence for a time before Beck spoke again.

"Well, it took some fancy talkin', but I've convinced the grand masters to be a little more ... forgivin' with Brennan. More forgivin' than usual, that is."

"The usual is him being dead, right?" Riley asked, looking over at him now.

"Yeah. I asked them to give Brennan a second chance. I felt he deserved it because he was in over his head, and I know how that goes. It's only fair since I got a second chance myself."

"We both did," she said softly. "Thanks for standing up for him. I'm really proud of you."

Beck shrugged, but she could see color creep onto his cheeks now, as if he was embarrassed. "Kepler's gonna tell the cops that Brennan was under a spell," he continued. "That should help keep him from bein' charged."

Riley pondered on that as they walked along the ridge overlooking the loch. She'd have to come back to Scotland for the trial. Which wouldn't be a bad thing if Beck was still here, but if he was already home it'd be a hassle.

"Once Brennan's healed up, they're bringin' him back here, makin' him finish his trainin' so he can head to Mexico when he's done. But you can bet they'll watch him damned close. One foot wrong and he's history."

Riley nodded her understanding. The grand masters were fair, but ruthless when they needed to be. *Like I'm much different.* After all, she'd just threatened two senior necromancers.

They chose a spot that had an unobstructed view and sat on a broad stone overlooking the loch.

"It's like there's no one else in the whole world but us," she said, speaking softly as if they were in church.

"Sometimes I wish that was the way it was. No demons. No necros. Just you and me."

She laid her head on Beck's shoulder as it continued to snow.

"I know I've kept things from you in the past," he said, "so ... ask me anythin' you want. If I can answer it, I will."

They really were starting over.

Riley went to the one thing that still dug at her like a jagged thorn, though she should have let it go. She sat up, looking him in straight in the eyes.

"Why Justine Armando? Of all the girls you could have slept with, why *that* one?"

Beck laughed, brown eyes dancing. "She still gets to you, doesn't she?"

"Just answer the question, please."

His laughter faded away. "I went with her because she was smokin' hot, the kind of woman I never figured I'd ever get to spend time with. Deep down, I knew she was usin' me, but it felt right at the time."

"Like me and Ori, then," Riley replied. "I was mad at you, and he said all the right things and I believed him."

"Yeah, him," Beck grumbled. "He really was tryin' to keep you safe." He stood, then took a few steps away, his back to her, lost in thought.

"Beck? Are you okay?"

"It depends on how the next few minutes go." Beck turned toward her, then went down on one knee. Again.

"Riley–" he began.

Before he had a chance to go any further, she launched herself at him and they fell back in the snow. She peered down at his astonished face.

"Yes!" she said. "I will marry you, Denver Beck."

He blinked a couple times. "For real?"

She nodded enthusiastically.

A rebel yell came next, along with a fist pump. Then he settled down, gazing deep in her eyes. "I love you, girl."

"I love you, too." She tapped his chin, thoughtfully. "If we're going to get married, I need you to promise that if anything happens to me, you'll go on. That you won't give up. Won't go climb in a bottle."

Beck held his breath for a moment, then exhaled, the snow still filtering down around them. "I don't know if I can promise that, Riley. I'm not as strong as you are."

"That's not true," she said. "You're not the same guy you were a few months ago. You're way stronger. I see it in everything you do."

"I don't know about that," he replied, shaking his head. "I can't imagine what it would be like without the woman I love."

Her heart melted, but she couldn't give this up. It was too important.

"Stewart felt the same way," she said. "You know how much he misses his wife, but he keeps doing his job, trying to make a difference. That's why I want you to promise not to give up, no matter what."

Beck thought it through, his brows furrowed. "Then you have to promise the same to me, that you'll keep going if I'm not around."

Could she? Riley swallowed hard at the thought of losing him.

"I agree. We both go on, no matter what," she said.

They sealed their vows with a kiss. Then he muttered something under his breath and pushed them into a sitting position. After digging in his coat pocket, a small box came her way.

"What's this?"

He popped it open, revealing a ring, the one she'd seen in Edinburgh at the street market.

"But … it's … a…"

Beck removed the ring, stashed the box away, and took hold of her left hand. With a tug her glove came free and he carefully threaded the ring onto the proper finger. It fit perfectly, the single red stone encircled by the ivy carved into the silver.

"But…" she tried again, still at a loss for words.

"My grandmamma's ring is for when we get married," he explained. "This one is to let the world know that yer *my* girl now, and nobody ever better mess with you."

He watched her process all that as the glint of tears filled her eyes.

"Oh, Den, it's so beautiful," she said.

"Like you," he whispered. "That's why I was late gettin' you at the nail place – I bought it and took it to a jeweler so he could check it over and clean it up."

Riley held up her hand to study the ring. "Can we afford this? I mean…"

"It wasn't that bad, and I've been savin' up since last spring." He cracked a grin. "I always hoped this day would come."

She looked up into his eyes, her own brimming with tears now. "You're so good to me."

"No more than you are to me, Riley."

Her smile thinned. "I'm so sorry I didn't say yes the first time."

Beck shook his head, no longer angry at what had happened between them. It didn't matter now.

"That wasn't yer fault." He gestured at the loch, the dark water against the pristine white snow. "This place feels right, like it was supposed to happen here. You know what I mean?"

She nodded. "Our own special place."

He stood, dusted the snow off his jeans and then offered his hand. "Come on, let's get back to the house before it gets dark. I want to tell the whole world yer mine now, and we'd best start with the masters. Fair warnin' though, I suspect there might be some whisky involved. In fact, I can promise that."

She chuckled as she rose and began to tug on her gloves. Beck had walked only a few paces away when he realized Riley wasn't with him. Right before he turned to check on her, a snowball hit him square on the butt.

He whirled around. "Hey!"

"That wasn't hard to hit," she said, grinning devilishly as she echoed something he said to her months before.

Beck blinked in surprise. "That was just luck."

His fiancé's reply was another snowball that struck him hard, mid-chest.

"Yer payin' for that one!"

He scooped up some ammunition of his own and the battle began. It was short lived, and in the end, they collapsed into each other's arms, laughing with unbridled joy.

"This is the way it's supposed to be," Riley said, pushing wet hair out of her eyes. "Less Hell. More fun."

"Then let's make sure to keep it that way, Princess."

"It's a deal, Backwoods Boy."

Chapter Fifteen

When the time came, Riley and Beck's farewell at the airport was bittersweet. She really wanted to stay with the guy she loved, but she needed to go home where there were apprentices to train, Latin classes to attend, friends missing her. That push-pull meant one moment there were tears, the next, homesickness.

Right before Riley entered the security line, she hesitated. "I wish you were coming home with me."

"Only a few more weeks," Beck said, brushing a strand of hair off her face. "Then we'll have more time together. Well, until I have come back here again. But soon I'll be home full time, you'll see."

Not soon enough.

That had been the other surprise he'd been holding back; he wasn't going to finish the grand master training by the end of the year. The fact that he read slower than most meant he was going to have to return after the holidays and stay until the end of February. Riley had tried hard not to cry, and had barely succeeded. At least she'd see him at Christmas, he'd said.

Now they shared one last fervent kiss, and then she reluctantly made her way through the security checkpoint. A secondary screening of her backpack took more time, but she didn't mind. It let her spend a bit more time with Beck, even if he wasn't right next to her.

After she'd been deemed "not a threat to aviation" Riley turned and waved at her guy. Beck waved back, his face so sad her heart clenched. She kept looking over her shoulder as she walked down the concourse and wasn't surprised he was watching her the entire time.

Just as she reached her gate, a text came through from Beck.

NEVER DOUBT I LOVE U.

Sinking into a seat near the window, Riley gave in and let the tears fall.

Epilogue

Four days after Riley returned to Atlanta she found herself headed down an alley in Little Five Points. On either side of her were doors of various colors, each home to either a witch or a summoner. This time she was visiting one of the latter, her dear friend Mortimer.

The young guy who answered the door had short brown hair and was dressed in worn jeans and a red tee-shirt. Unlike Mort's usual domestic help, he wasn't a reanimate.

"Oh, hi," he said, checking her out while leaning in the doorway. "You're Riley, right? Uncle Mort said you'd be coming by."

Uncle Mort?

Before she could reply, he continued. "I'm Alex," the boy said and waved her in. "I'm staying here for a while, taking time off before I start college."

That meant he was about her age, though he appeared older. "What's your major?"

"Physics."

"Okay, that's hardcore. I'm just taking a Latin course and that's totally kicking my butt."

"Latin, huh?" he said, smiling now. "No wonder my uncle thinks you're cool." Alex gestured down the hallway. "He's in his office. You know the way, right?"

Riley nodded and set off, recalling the first time she'd come here, how nervous she'd been. How during one visit she'd found her reanimated father waiting for her.

It seemed like decades ago.

The house wasn't any different – the same tasteful pictures on the walls – only she had changed.

When she entered Mort's office, a curiously circular room, he looked up from the picnic table that served as his desk.

"There you are," he said, beaming. Mort rose and they exchanged hugs. He was a short and wide fellow, but a good friend and the kind of dude you wanted watching your back.

"Beck sends his best," she said.

"Master Stewart says he's doing really well."

"He is. He'll make a fine grand master." She smiled at the thought.

"Good, this world needs people like him." Mort pointed at the ring at her hand. "I hear you two made it official."

Riley grinned, holding the ring up for closer scrutiny. "No complaints. It's all really good right now."

"And you want to ensure it stays that way," Mort hedged.

She sobered. "Yeah, that's exactly why I'm here."

They sat across from each other at the picnic table.

"You see, I have no real choice," she began. "The only way people are going to leave us alone is if we're so badass they won't touch us. Beck is doing his part by becoming a grand master, but I have to be just as strong or they'll keep messing with us. Someday ... we might not make it."

Mort nodded sagely. "I was wondering when you were going to come to that conclusion."

"It wasn't easy," Riley admitted, then nervously cleared her throat. "I can't spend the rest of my life having people dropping spells on my head, trying to use me as bait to summon angels, demons or the monster of the month. I need to learn..." She swallowed the lump in her throat. "I need to learn defensive magic."

Mort leaned forward on his elbows. "This is hard for you, isn't it? You never wanted to go down this path."

"No, I don't. I'm a trapper, not a summoner."

"Okay, then I won't teach you how to raise the dead, though you would be good at it."

"No way. Don't want to go there. Not after what happened to my dad."

He nodded his understanding. "Stewart told me you broke a compulsion spell while you were in Scotland. Put the summoner right on her butt. That means you know how to channel magic."

"Yes, but I don't know how I did it."

"You have an incredibly strong will," Mort replied, "and that's very important."

She wasn't sure about that.

"It seems that Lord Ozymandias had a very terse conversation with a summoner named Enfield. Her report of what happened over there has intrigued his lordship, to say the least."

That wasn't good news. "Did she tell them I threatened them?"

He chuckled. "Yes. His lordship found that very amusing. Oh, and word is that you won't be returning to Scotland for a trial."

"What? Why not?"

"Summoner Faye is dead. They placed a restraining spell on her. As long as she didn't try to do any magic, she was fine. Of course, she ignored their warning and tried to bespell her way out of jail. That was a very fatal mistake."

"Wow," Riley murmured. *She's dead.*

Which meant it was all over, since Bess had pled guilty to a lesser charge than kidnapping. Her lawyer had wisely pushed the "mitigating circumstances" defense, like the fact she thought her only daughter was dying. It had worked.

Riley pulled herself back to the present. "So how do we do this?" she asked, her palms suddenly sweaty. She wiped them on her jeans, but it didn't seem to help.

"I'll teach you the basics," Mort said. "Then Ozymandias will teach you the stronger protection spells."

"What? Oh no, I couldn't–" *Not him.*

"He's the best," Mort insisted. "I know you don't like him because of what he did to your father, but if you want to keep you and Beck safe, it's the smartest way. Besides the new Ozy isn't like the old one. I think you'll be surprised. He actually has a sense of humor, believe it or not."

It was the first time she'd ever heard Mort shorten the high lord's name. Apparently her friend was loosening up. Or Ozy was.

"I'm not sure about him," she admitted.

"Then we'll tackle that problem when we get to it. You ready to dig in today, or do you want to wait?"

Riley thought of Beck in Scotland. Of his smile, of his unconditional love. How she wanted all that for the rest of her life, no matter what it cost.

"Today works for me," she announced.

"Okay then, we'll start with the basics. Put your palms flat on the table."

Riley did as she was told, nervous, as Mort collected a candle, lit it and then placed it in front of her. He settled back on the bench seat.

"Focus on the candle flame. Let it fill you."

As she let the light enter her mind and her heart, she heard her father's soft voice. *I am so proud of you.*

She smiled to herself and focused harder.

This is for you, Den. For us. For our future.

Thank You!

Thanks for reading *Grave Matters*. I sincerely hope that you enjoyed it.

On the following pages you will find some BONUS CONTENT which includes demon illustrations and two *Demon Trapper* short stories. Please be sure to check them out.

Reviews allow other readers to find my books. If you could help me get the word out about *Grave Matters,* that would be great. Please tell other Demon Trappers fans about the novella, post reviews (either positive or negative) on Goodreads and the various online booksellers' sites, etc. I would really appreciate it.

If you've never read the other books in the Demon Trappers series, please check out the following websites for details:

www.DemonTrappers.com

www.DemonTrappers.co.uk

If you'd like to stay in touch with me about new books, guest appearances and just about everything else:

Facebook: www.Facebook.com/janaoliver
Twitter: @crazyauthorgirl
Or at my website: www.JanaOliver.com

Thank you for sharing in another Riley and Beck adventure!

Bonus Content

Demon Illustrations
by Mark Helwig

Denver Beck Short Story
Personal Demons

Riley Blackthorne Short Story
Retro Demonology

Klepto-Fiend

by Mark Helwig

Grade One Demon

Biblio-Fiend

by Mark Helwig

Grade One Demon

Gastro-Fiend

by Mark Helwig

Grade Three Demon

Archfiend

by Mark Helwig

Personal Demons

A Denver Beck Short Story

**Set three years before the first book
in the Demon Trappers Series**

*August 2015
Atlanta, Georgia*

Denver Beck knew he had to prove himself on this run, or call it quits. Every apprentice demon trapper faced this test: today he would trap his first Grade Three demon. If he succeeded, he would be one step closer to becoming a journeyman trapper. If not, he'd have proved so many people right – that he was nothing more than a waste of space.

For the last few months he'd been under the watchful eye of a master demon trapper, learning the ins and outs of the trade. In truth, Paul Blackthorne was more like a father than a teacher, a role that began when they'd first met in Paul's high school history class. Beck had always respected the man, an easy-going widower in his early forties. Even after Paul had lost his teaching job and become a demon trapper, their friendship continued. Now it was Beck's chance to show him just how good he could be.

Though Hellspawn could be found anywhere in Atlanta, they liked to congregate in the Five Points area just south of downtown. The trappers, a mismatched crew of men from all walks of life, called it Demon Central. It was the best place to find one of Lucifer's more ferocious Hellspawn, a Gastro-Fiend. Threes, as the trappers called them, were dedicated killings machines.

He and Paul had been called out to trap such a beast. As they descended the first of three lengthy escalators into the depths of Peachtree station, Beck shifted the strap of his heavy trapping bag to keep it from digging into his shoulder. It was loaded with the usual trapper supplies: a two foot length of steel pipe, a bag of chicken entrails, magical spheres and a few bottles of Holy Water. With the heat, the chicken was beginning to smell.

From below them came the characteristic whine of one of the trains entering the station. Though the city was bankrupt, the MARTA trains kept running, though erratically. The Peachtree station was on one of the main railway lines, located underground in the heart of the city.

The August heat made his tee shirt stick to his skin. Beck skimmed a hand through his military-style short blond hair. He had a history with this particular station and it hadn't been a good one. The last time he'd been here he'd tried to trap a Pyro-Fiend, a fire-loving demon. He'd seriously botched the capture and a Hazardous Materials (Hazmat) team had been summoned to deal with the cleanup. Both he and Paul had taken a lot of grief from the Demon Trappers Guild for that screw up. It had nearly cost him his apprentice licence.

If he screwed up this time, he was history.

Why am I doin' this? I gotta be crazy. Unfortunately there wasn't much else a twenty-year-old veteran could do unless he wanted to break the law, or live on the streets.

A kid on the opposite escalator let out a war hoop and Beck instinctively crouched down, his heart pounding and his mouth dry. When he realized the source of the noise, he rose to his feet, feeling like a fool.

He'd only been home from the Middle East for a few months. Everyday noises, the kind that other people ignored, he had to process through his war-heightened senses. He found himself automatically scanning faces, looking for enemies, folks who might want to shoot him in the back or trigger a cache of explosives.

In Afghanistan, that extreme caution had saved his life. Though the war was supposedly winding down, there was always someone who'd love to kill a bunch of Americans, especially if they wore uniforms. On one afternoon, a roadside bomb had come very close to killing him.

No matter how he tried, Beck was still too keyed up to let down his guard.

His mentor noticed. "The only bad guys here are the demons," Paul said softly. "No need to be so jumpy."

"I can't help myself. It's the way I am right now."

"It's not a bad habit, Den," Paul continued, "it's just that it takes your attention away from the real threats." His friend smiled at him. "Don't worry, you'll do fine."

"Glad one of us thinks so."

The Guild categorized demons according to their lethality and their general intelligence. Fortunately Gastro-Fiends weren't that bright, but they made up for that with pure ferocity. Threes stood at about four feet tall, their bodies covered in fur, usually solid black. The younger ones were plump and had a single row of teeth, both top and bottom. The mature ones had more teeth and highly aggressive.

Though Paul wouldn't let this thing eat him, but there was nothing to stop it from ripping out Beck's entrails before his friend nailed it with a Holy Water sphere.

"The fiend could be hiding in the tunnels or on one of the trains," Paul remarked, always in teacher mode. "How do you propose we find it?"

"Listen for the screams?" Beck joked.

"Sometimes it isn't that easy."

Then the screaming began.

"Ah, damn!" Beck said and took off at a trot, hurrying past other passengers on the escalator. Once he and Paul reached the platform, they found a knot of civilians all trying to get somewhere else in a hurry. The reason for their panic was about ten yards away – a Gastro-Fiend. This one was leaner, with thick muscles underneath the rank fur, and it sported two crooked layers of teeth. Six talons protruded from each paw and its eyes were laser red.

He'd seen them before, but Paul had been the one trapping them. Now this was his.

"It's one of the older ones," Paul warned. 'It'll move faster than you're used to. Keep it away from the civilians and I'll hit it with the Holy Water."

Beck's hands shook as he eased his trapping bag to the concrete.

Adrenalin stormed through his body and he forced himself to take a deep breath. This was the part of the job that scared the hell out of him, and the part he lived for.

"You be careful, okay?" Paul said.

"Yes, sir," Beck replied. He quickly removed pipe and the entrails, which would serve as bait. Paul already had a Holy Water sphere in hand, ready to deliver it the moment the demon went after Beck. If he hit the fiend in the face with the glass sphere, it would be rendered unconscious long enough to secure it. It wasn't a perfect take-down system, but it usually worked. When it didn't, trappers got hurt… or killed.

No longer fascinated with a trash container's contents, the demon had taken an unholy interest in a teenage boy. The kid was busily snapping photos of the monster with his cell phone, no doubt to impress his friends.

Idiot! "Get the hell away from it!" Beck shouted, already on the move.

Startled, the teen peered over his shoulder at him, a deer in the headlights. The fiend chose that moment to launch its attack.

Beck picked up speed, legs pumping in a bid to cover the distance in half the time. As he ran, he heaved the bag of entrails so it landed some distance to the left of the kid. The Three ignored it, homing in on the much larger meal.

Shouting to attract its attention, Beck put himself between the teen and the Three. He hip-checked the boy toward an open train car.

"Go!" he shouted.

The kid stumbled, hit the floor of the train and slid, his fingers still locked around the phone. Though the civilian was out of the way, Beck found himself out of position. He tried to turn fast enough to ward off the demon, but it raked his arm with its toxic claws as it charged by. He bellowed in pain.

With a startling crash, a Holy Water sphere shattered against the side of the train, splattering liquid and glass fragments in all directions. It'd just missed the demon's head.

To Beck's relief, the car doors closed and the train rolled of the station.

At least the kid's safe.

Its departure distracted the fiend long enough for Beck to back away and assess the situation. The Three was doing the same as drool rolled down its chin. It glared at him with flame-red eyes. He flinched at the sight of his blood and flesh on the thing's claws.

Beck tightened his grip on the pipe. It felt warm to the touch.

"Trapperrr!" the demon cried as it flung itself at Beck. He slammed at it with his pipe, but his timing was off. Instead of a solid blow, the Three hooked a paw around the weapon, using it to pull him closer. Before he realized what was happening, its teeth snapped inches from his neck, its foul breath scorching him as the stink of putrid fur filled his nose.

A glass sphere slammed into the demon's shoulder, but it had no effect. Beck released the pipe and lurched to the side. Instead of dropping it, the demon sent the weapon flying across the open space directly at him. When he raised an arm to shield himself, it bounced off the bone, clipping his forehead as it passed. Beck's head exploded in a burst of pain and he almost went to his knees. If he did, he was dead.

"Get out of the way!" Paul called out, panic in his voice now.

When Beck complied with the order, another Holy Water sphere flew through the air, but it missed. He grabbed up the pipe, but the fiend was already on the move, taking a running leap at him. They tumbled onto the concrete and rolled, their combined momentum carrying them off the platform into the dirty pit below.

He landed hard on his back, the wind knocked out of him, costing him precious seconds to regain his breath. Looking around wildly, he cursed when he saw that his pipe hadn't made the journey with him. He also realized he was next to the covered rail, the one that supplied the electricity to run the trains. He quickly scooted away from it.

No wonder Paul hadn't thrown another sphere, not with Beck so close to that massive power source. Get fried was never his idea of fun.

"Den?" his friend called out, his face peering over the edge of the platform. "You okay?"

Beck gave a nod and pulled up himself up, searching for the demon. It was about fifteen feet away, rising to its clawed feet as well. He was pleased to see it had taken some hurt: one arm was cut and dripping black blood.

A low rumble filled the station as a train arrived on the other side of the platform. That meant there were more people now, more chances for someone to get hurt. The demon raised its muzzle and sniffed the air, scenting fresh prey.

Beck backed away slowly. He was out of weapons, and if he ran, the fiend would just chase him down and rip him apart. If the demon followed him onto the platform, it'd get worse in a hurry. From there it had a couple ways to escape and a lot of people it could damage in the process. Even though the MARTA cops were trying to clear out the curious, folks weren't moving. Not when there was so much drama.

I have to keep it down here with me.

Beck became aware that his friend stood just to his left, up on the platform.

"This pretty much blows, Paul," he called out.

"I agree. I don't have a good shot right now, not with you down there."

"I know and if I crawl out, the demon will follow me right into the civilians."

Paul turned and shouted at one of the MARTA cops, pleading with them to clear the platform. They were doing their best, but some of the passengers refused to leave, their cell phones out, just in case this turned out to be a graphic YouTube moment.

A plan began to form in Beck's mind. "Give me my pipe and a sphere," he called out.

"Water isn't your friend right now," Paul warned.

"I know," he replied. It wasn't the demon's, either.

The requested items came his way, along with his friend's worried muttering. Beck tucked the orb up close to his chest, and brandished the pipe.

The demon shifted it weight forward, a sign it was about to

make another run.

"Chew yourrrr bones!" it yelled as it rushed him.

Beck struck it hard in the chest, and again, the thing clawed him as it passed, coming dangerously close.

Ah, hell.

Beck spun around and backed away, never having had the chance to use the sphere.

Maybe this isn't a good idea after all.

As the train on the other side of the platform began to move out of the station, Beck shot a look over the demon's shoulder. It was only a matter of time before one arrived on their tracks. Maybe he could use that to his advantage.

He glanced up at the electronic billboard, hoping to see when the next train would arrive. The board was running an ad for some concert.

"Damn," he muttered.

The demon was breathing heavily now and glancing repeatedly toward Paul and the platform. Instead of taking him down, was it weighing its chances of escape?

It was time to get the thing mad. If it was trying to kill him, it wouldn't be thinking clearly.

"Hey, demon, how's this goin' for ya?" Beck called out. "Yer the best old Lucifer's got?" He snorted. "No wonder they kicked his sorry ass out of Heaven."

The fiend snarled at the mention of its master's name. They hated being reminded they were nothing more than Hell's slaves.

"Come on, dumbass. Let's get this done. Or are ya afraid of one little trapper?"

The demon roared its anger, waving its arms in the air.

Now!

He sent the pipe end over end toward the Three's head. It ducked, which was exactly what Beck had hoped. He ran forward, under-handing the sphere directly into the demon's face. The sphere shattered, splattering the sacred liquid. With a groan, the monster crumpled onto its knees between the tracks, fighting to stay conscious.

A low noise brought Beck's eyes up as a train loomed out of the tunnel on his tracks, so close he felt the pressure wave of air that rode just ahead of it.

"Den! Get out of there!" Paul cried.

Beck took a desperate leap toward the platform, his knees ramming into side of it as he tried to claw his way out. The horn split the air, followed by the shriek of brakes as the train operator realized the tracks weren't empty.

Hands grabbed at him and pulled. Beck felt something tug on the back of one of his boots, nearly pulling it off. A high-pitched cry filled the air. For a second he thought it had come from his mouth. There was a sickening crunch and then the sound of fat sparks.

After what seemed an eternity, he slumped like a beached whale, belly first, on the concrete platform.

When the train halted, Beck forced himself to breath. "My legs… are they still there?" He knew how massive injuries sometimes didn't register right off. He'd learned that one personally.

Paul checked him over as he knelt next to him. "You're good. I don't see anything missing. Where does it hurt?"

"Everywhere," Beck mumbled. He sighed. It had been the train tugging on one of his boots. It'd been too close. With considerable effort, he slowly raised his head. "The Three?"

"It's history," Paul replied in between deep breaths, his eyes were wide. He was shaking and that spooked Beck more than anything. "Oh God, Den, your back's all ripped up."

Tell me about it.

Beck placed his cheek on the cool concrete as all his wounds sent frantic *ohmigod it hurts* messages to his overloaded brain. At least he wasn't train sushi like the demon.

The air slowly filled with the sickening stench of burning fur as around them came excited voices and the crackle of police radios.

Eventually, with Paul's help, Beck sat upright, which only made his back throb in time to the wound in his scalp. He took a grim inventory: the adrenalin surge was making him sick to his stomach, his hands and knees were skinned and there was too much blood on his jeans and the front of his tee shirt to be good news.

"Fire department and Hazmat are rolling," one of the MARTA cops exclaimed.

Ah shit. Not again.

As someone gagged in response to the stench of roasting demon, an announcement came over the intercom stating that the north-south MARTA line was out of service for the time being. That was going to piss off some folks, especially those headed to the airport.

And I'm to blame. All he'd wanted was to make Paul proud of him, but like most things in his life, it'd gone square to hell. *Maybe I should just give it up now.*

Paul rose and flipped open his license as a cop approached. "I'm Master Trapper Blackthorne and this is my apprentice. We were called here to deal with a Grade Three demon."

"That's not what we heard," the man replied, frowning. "We got a report of some crazy person was playing tag with a demon and throwing people onto the tracks."

Beck kept his mouth shut and let his mentor take the lead. He had too much of a temper and if he let it loose, it'd only get worse. If that was possible.

Despite his friend's even-tempered approach it took Paul five minutes of calm reassurances to get the cops to understand that they weren't the enemy. That didn't stop the "protect and serve" crowd from having the bomb squad's dog check out both their trapping bags and themselves. There had never been any love lost between the trappers and the cops.

When the dog sniffed at Beck, it backed off, sneezing. With a whine it ducked behind its handler's legs.

"I've never seen him do that before," the guy said.

"Dogs are smart – they fear demons, and right now that's what my partner smells like," Paul explained.

The bomb squad dude took his canine elsewhere.

As it all played out, thin oily smoke continued to fill the cavern, the remains of fried Three polluting the air and everyone close to it. Beck watched with no amusement as the fire department and the Hazmat guys tried to figure out how to handle the situation. He was willing to bet there was nothing in their manuals for that one.

What an effin' mess.

Paul helped him limp to the nearest wooden bench and then sat next to him, a bottle of Holy Water in hand.

"Just do it," Beck said. He'd only get sicker if the wounds weren't treated soon, the toxins causing his body to rot from the inside out.

When the sacred liquid hit his clawed-up leg, Beck bit off an oath, mindful they were in public. Next came the arm and finally his back. The latter's searing agony nearly made him vomit.

"That'll hold until the doctor can patch you up," Paul announced, tucking the empty bottle in his trapping bag. "God, you took a lot of damage."

"It don't matter anyway," Beck said, his voice tight. "Master Harper was right – I'm a total loser. He's gonna make sure they toss my ass out of the Guild for this. Maybe I should just save them the trouble and walk away now."

Paul was suddenly in his face. "What? I thought you were tougher than that, Den. You always said you were. Was that just bullshit or did that demon slice off your balls, too?"

Beck reared back, stunned. He'd never heard his friend talk like that. "Don't act like this isn't a big deal. That kid's parents are gonna sue the hell out of me and the Guild. This is seriously fuc–"

"It isn't a picnic, and it's never easy, but what you're doing is important. You saved that boy's life, and now you think it isn't worth it?"

"But I screwed up."

"We all do. That's life." His friend frowned. "So what's it going to be? Are you in or out? Tell me now. I have to know."

If he quit, Beck knew what the other trappers would say. *Yeah, he gave it up. Didn't have the guts to make it. Never was one of us.* Then they'd say he wasn't man enough to handle the job.

"Den, are you in or are you out?" his friend asked solemnly.

Paul deserved an answer.

Beck weighed his future and took a gamble. "I'm in," he murmured, so softly he wondered if he actually said the words.

Paul sighed in relief. "So tell me, what did you do wrong?"

"Everythin'?"

'No, not quite. The next time you trap a Three you're need to be a lot smarter, providing you learned something from this... disaster. So talk to me. Tell me what you would have done differently."

Let some other dumbass capture the thing?

Knowing that comment was only going to buy him grief, Beck worked back through the trapping, step by step. "I shoulda been carryin' a sphere right up front, since I was gonna be so close to that thing."

A nod returned. "What else?"

"I shoulda given ya a clear field of fire. I was in the way most of the time so ya couldn't hit the demon."

"Correct. And... ?"

He looked over at his mentor. "What else is there?"

"Do not play chicken with a train," Paul replied, his tone sharper now. "That was just crazy, Den."

"Yeah, well, it kept the demon away from the civilians."

"Yes, it did. It was also remarkably brave. I don't know if I'd have had the guts to do that."

"The Guild isn't gonna see it that way."

"They might once they view the security footage," Paul replied. "That could save our butts."

Beck hadn't considered that. Everything he'd done would have been recorded.

"That's a damn long shot and ya know it."

"That's the story of our lives. One long shot after another."

That could save our butts. He looked away, staring into the distance. This wasn't just about him. *What will they do to Paul? They wouldn't kick him out of the Guild because of me, would they?*

Beck didn't dare ask the question. He noticed a burly man talk his way through the ring of MARTA cops and head their way. He had a linebacker's build and wore a dark suit and blue tie. His expression was no-nonsense.

"You the trapper who tossed my kid inside a train?" he demanded, his eyes on Beck. His voice was deep and resonant.

Here it comes. "Yes, sir, I am." No reason not to take the heat.

"Get up here, son," he ordered. The teen who'd put himself

in harm's way shuffled up, one of his high top's laces untied. He puffed hard like he'd been running. The boy stared at the floor, his cell phone in hand as if was a permanent part of his anatomy. "So what do you tell this guy, Billy?"

"Ah…" The boy looked up at Beck. "Thanks. What you did was… awesome."

"Yer okay?"

"Yeah," he said, smiling. "I ran back from Five Points station to see what happened. I even got some of it on my phone."

"I'm sure ya did." Beck winced as he tried to sit straighter. "Just promise me ya'll keep away from those things, ya hear?"

"Yes, sir. I won't get near one again."

Sir? Beck found that amusing. He wasn't more than about four years older than this boy and yet it felt like at least fifty.

"Then it's all good," he murmured. *At least for the kid.*

"My son called me and told me what happened," the man explained. "You saved his life. I won't forget that."

"That's our job, sir," Beck said.

The man handed Paul a business card. "Let me know if this young fellow needs anything, okay?"

"I will. Thank you, Mr … Dennis."

The guy nodded, then headed off toward the exit, the teen in tow.

Paul chuckled as he stuck the card in a shirt pocket. "You know, Den, you must have an angel watching over you."

'Why would ya think that?'

"That gentleman works in the governor's office. He's the ombudsman." At Beck's puzzled expression he added, "He's the kind of guy you want in your corner if this gets ugly with the Guild."

"Really?" His friend nodded. "Well, hell…"

It took some effort for Paul to get him to his feet. To his embarrassment, Beck found he was dizzy, his head whirling around like he'd downed a six pack way too fast.

"And I wanted to be a trapper…why?" he muttered.

"As I remember, you said it'd help you score with the chicks,"

Paul said, grinning.

"Riiiight. Shows what I know."

They'd barely made it through the turnstile on the upper level when someone stepped in their path.

Beck groaned. He knew the guy – George something or other – a reporter for one of the local TV stations who'd covered his last major screw-up.

"Hey, Beck. What is it with you and train stations?" the guy said, grinning. "Here I thought it was going to be a slow news day." He waved a finger in the air and the cameraman behind him clicked on the lights and began filming.

"We're live in Peachtree MARTA station," the reporter began, "where a heroic rescue as just taken place."

"I am not a hero," Beck grumbled under his breath.

Paul's elbow clipping his ribs told him now was not the time to be humble.

"Master Blackthorne, can you give us a rundown of what happened today?"

The microphone came his way. "I most certainly can."

Paul always has my back. Why would I ever walk away from this guy?

~ ~ ~ ~ ~

When Beck finally made it to street level, he slumped on a bench while Paul went to collect the car. He gulped in the fresh air, though he could still smell the roasting demon on his clothes. His teeth were starting to chatter as a fever took hold, even though his injuries had been treated with Holy Water. As time went on, the demon wounds wouldn't bother him as much, but right now he was getting the full Hellish treatment.

As least I'm not a grease spot on the tracks.

As he gloomily pondered the odds of keeping his job, two small feet appeared close to his blood-stained boots. He looked up to find a little girl, maybe four years of age, watching him intently. He tried to smile, but even his lips hurt.

"Hi," he said, his voice thick.

"Hi," she replied. She had big brown eyes and brown hair, which sort of reminded him of Paul's daughter. This little one could be a mini Riley, though her nose was shorter and her eyes were more green than brown.

After a look at her mom, probably for courage, the girl offered him a small ice cream cone. "I saw what you did. Sworry you're hurt," she said with a slight lisp.

"Thanks. That's mighty kind of ya," he said and took the gift, hoping the kid didn't notice the blood on his hands.

She skittered back to her parents, suddenly shy. Her dad gave him a thumbs up, which Beck returned, and then they walked away, the little girl holding their hands and talking animatedly.

At least someone likes me.

He'd even scored a vanilla cone out of the deal. He took a long lick and let the cool creaminess melt inside his mouth. It tasted pretty good. Besides, he'd always been a sucker for a cute smile.

Maybe his life didn't suck as bad as he thought. He was doing what he loved, even if the job kept trying to kill him. If the Guild ruled in his favour – and that would be a miracle – someday he'd be a journeyman, even a master demon trapper just like Paul.

No, this wasn't the end of his career.

Maybe this is just the beginnin'.

Retro Demonology

Riley's First Solo Trapping

****Set a few weeks before the first book
in the Demon Trappers Series****

Atlanta
January 2018

The *Proud to Be Retro* decal on the house's front door should
have been Riley Blackthorne's first clue, but then every day was
bizarre when you were an apprentice Demon Trapper. She double-
checked the address on the trapping order clutched in her left
hand. This was the place.

Just my luck.

Retro was gaining favor in Atlanta, what with the economy
fizzling like a damp firecracker and the city bankrupt. When today
sucked, why not "live" in a simpler, more perfect time? Even if that
time had actually sucked as bad as this one. Some Retros preferred
the 1980's, some the '40s. Exactly which era this client had chosen
remained to be seen.

"Please, not the '50s again," Riley murmured. A couple weeks
back, she and her demon trapper dad had encountered a Retro
lady with her head firmly in 1955. She'd been clad in a pink and
white floral dress, a white starched apron, heels and a single strand
of pearls. She had a picture of Dwight D. Eisenhower on her wall
and her kitchen was all white metal cabinets, chrome chairs and
linoleum. She'd been one very mad Retro lady by the time they'd
fished a swearing, peeing and biting demon from amidst her prized
cookbook collection. Though the mess on her pristine cabinets and
floor wasn't anything major, Ms. '50s acted like it was the end of
the world. And told them so. . .repeatedly.

As Riley's father had said after the incident, "Sometimes I like
the demons more than the clients."

With a silent prayer heavenward, Riley rapped on the weathered door. Fidgeting, she straightened her jeans jacket and flipped her long brown hair behind her shoulders. Up to this point her father had watched over her on each trapping run, preventing her from making seriously dumb moves. Today there was no dad backup and that made her off-the-scale nervous. No, she couldn't expect special treatment just because her father was Paul Blackthorne, legendary master trapper.

That was the way it was done – the master took the newbie on trapping runs until he deemed the apprentice was ready to handle the smaller demons on his (or in Riley's case) her own. Once she'd passed that test, they'd tackle the next grade level of Hellspawn, on and on until she took down a Grade Five Geo-Fiend. But that would be at least six months away. Once she'd completed her training, she'd take a test and become a journeyman trapper. A lot was riding on this gig, if nothing more than to prove to the other trappers in the Atlanta Guild she wasn't some silly wannabe.

The door creaked open and a woman peered out at her. She looked about forty, but was trying to look younger, with a blonde Afro, hip hugger bell bottoms, a bunch of beads and a black *Peace Now* tee shirt. More troubling: her eyes didn't focus right.

Oh crap. She's into the '60s. Her dad had warned her about these folks. Another face appeared – this belonged to a stick thin guy with shoulder-length brown hair held back by a black bandana across his forehead. A bushy beard, tee shirt advocating free love and ratty jeans left no doubt he was way into the late 1960s. Both of them wore sandals with no socks. In January.

"Peace," the woman said, then made the appropriate sign with her two fingers. The guy did the same.

Clearly Riley was going to have to be the adult in this conversation.

"I'm here to take care of your ..." She hesitated at this point. Her dad had taught her to *never* say the "d" word in public until the client was willing to acknowledge that they had a fiendish issue. Demons in your home rated right up there with declaring your place a plague pit. Some people wouldn't buy a house if there'd ever been a fiend inside. "I'm here to take care of your *problem*."

The pair just stared at her.

"You know. *The* problem?" Nothing. So much for subtlety. "I'm a Demon Trapper."

"Oh, groovy," the woman said and smiled. Riley decided she was probably called Sunflower or something like that given her oversize hairstyle. "The Man at the Guild said you'd like have this piece of paper."

Maybe she means my license. Riley dug in her messenger bag and produced the apprentice Demon Trapper license, laminated proof that she was allowed to capture Hellspawn. Well, at least the small ones. Mini demons loved to steal jewelry, destroy books, burn out circuit boards and stick dead roaches inside denture cups. It was all annoying stuff. Unless you were a denture wearer or a librarian.

As Riley offered up the license the photograph mocked her. Back when it'd been taken her hair had been this amazing blend of brown and black with bright teal highlights. Now it was her natural brown because her dad had insisted on it. "People judge by appearances," he'd said. "You need to look like a pro. Blue hair doesn't cut it."

Neither does dull brown.

"You're only seventeen?" Sunflower asked, raising a blonde eyebrow.

"Yes, but I'm fully trained to handle Grade One demons," Riley replied, just like her father had taught her when the age issue arose.

"He's a majorly wacked out," Bandana announced. "He crossed the line."

"What line?" Riley asked, puzzled.

"He went after Jim's albums," the guy said, shaking his head in disgust. "That's so not cool."

"We tried to get him to split, check out someone's pad, but he won't go," the woman added. "So we called The Man."

Don't try to make sense of this. Just get it done.

The license was returned, then she was led through a house populated with garish orange and green bean bag chairs, bead curtains and a Che Guevara poster. Some sort of East Indian music played in the background. Worse, the place reeked of patchouli. Riley sneezed. Twice. Then dug for a tissue.

I just have to snag the demon and make a break for it. Then run her clothes through the washer a few times so they didn't smell like she lived in a Buddhist monastery.

They entered a room at the back of the house that looked like a shrine. Probably because it was. One full wall was covered in posters, all of this particular band. In the middle of them was a huge picture of this cute guy with shaggy brown hair, clothed in a leather jacket, and holding a microphone. Beneath the picture was a plaque that said *Light My Fire* 1943-1971. Then there were the rows and rows of candles that sent pinpoints of light onto the remaining tapestry-covered walls.

This has to be a setup. My dad must have talked a couple of his buddies into messing with my head. Yeah, it's a hazing.

She waited for the "Gotcha" moment from the pair of hippies. It didn't come.

"See?" Sunflower asked.

All Riley saw was serious obsession with Jim Morrison and *The Doors*. Her father had been a fan, but this was way more than that.

"Neat room," Riley said, figuring that was a safe response.

"No, not that," Sunflower exclaimed. "See?"

Following the woman's pointed finger, Riley finally spied the demon on the altar, perched next to a small statue of the Jim guy.

"Can you dig it?" Sunflower asked in a jangle of beads.

"Yeah, I got it," Riley said.

Trappers had a rating scale for demons based on how dangerous they were: Grade One to Grade Five. This was a One, a Biblio-Fiend. It might be small, but it could rip through a library like a chainsaw when it was in the proper mood. Which was pretty much all the time.

As Riley slowly moved forward to study the fiend, it cut loose a string of swear words. It was about three inches tall, had pointed ears and was mocha in color. The most unnerving feature was its two brilliant red eyes which glowered at her menacingly.

"Trappperr ..." it hissed, then swore again.

The little demon did have two other weapons besides its foul personality: sharp teeth and. . . She backed off just in time to avoid a tiny stream of green urine that came her way. No way did she want it to wreck her jeans.

This kind hated books, but that didn't explain why it was here. This wasn't a library or a bookstore, yet something had attracted it. There was a topped pile of New Age books on the floor near the altar, but nothing that compelling unless you wanted to read about composting, aligning your chakras, or five-toed Chinese dragons.

As she watched, the thing tugged a book from underneath its butt and began to rip out the pages. She caught a glimpse of the spine. The book was by John Milton.

"Ah, that's your problem," Riley said, relieved to be on familiar ground. "You've got a copy of *Paradise Lost* in your house. Biblios hate Milton. Same with Dante, C.S. Lewis and most holy books. They'll go after those every time."

"So, like, how do we get the dude to bug out?" Bandana asked.

Riley turned toward the pair. They couldn't be like this all the time, could they? "I have a secret weapon," she replied, trying hard to sound confident. That's not how she felt.

Wish my dad was here.

There was the sound of another page ripping free. This time the demon made it into a spit ball and launched the missile at her. It plonked off her forehead.

Glowering at the little fiend, she tried to think this through. That was paramount – the trapper must retain control of the trapping.

Warnings. I haven't done those yet. She hadn't memorized those completely, so she pulled the Unintended Consequences and Perils sheet out of her messenger bag and began to run down the list. As she read off the potential hazards, the clients clustered around her.

"They steal souls? Now that's gnarly," Bandana said, pointing to one of the listed perils. Most of which didn't apply to the demon on the altar.

"Talk about a drag," the woman replied.

Riley finished the list and then sighed in relief as Sunflower and her noisy beads signed the paperwork. Now she was free to get on with the trapping. She'd just opened her mouth to suggest that the pair take a hike, when Bandana guy said, "We'll just hang loose, stay out of your way."

"Yeah, we've got brownies in the oven," And then they were gone, shutting the door behind them.

Riley sighed in relief. Then she turned to eye her foe. The demon flipped her off in response. "What are you doing here with these people? Are you nuts?" she demanded.

It grinned, showing its teeth. And tore another page out of Milton.

"That does it."

Biblio-Fiends had a weakness: books. It's why they hated them. If a trapper read the right text to a Biblio, they went comatose and were easier to capture. Her father had told her that dense prose worked better than a hot romance novel. Riley didn't buy that, so she tried a steamy scene from *The Virgin Bride's Secret Greek Lover,* despite her dad's dire warnings. The results hadn't been pretty. It'd taken them over an hour to catch the enraged Biblio as it'd rampaged through the stacks of police procedurals and true crimes in a local bookstore.

Having learned her lesson, Riley extracted her weapon of choice: *Moby Dick.* She took a deep breath, opened the book to the first page and began to read.

"*Call me Ishmael.*" She continued the literary torture of Melville's convoluted prose. "*It is a way I have of driving off the spleen, and regulating the circulation.*' If she'd had an extra hand, her fingers would be crossed at this point.

There was a series of moans. "Boon I grant you, Blackthorne's daughter," the demon cried out, writhing in agony.

Riley kept reading. She knew that one boon led to another and another. The final payoff would be the Welcome to Hell lecture by none other than the Prince himself.

There was a sharp cry of anguish when she got to '*whenever it is a damp, drizzly November in my soul...*'. Then silence. Riley looked up from the page and grinned – the fiend had passed out.

"Trapper scores!" she said, shooting a fist into the air. Then she heard her father's voice just like he was standing next to her. "Don't count your Hellspawn before they're secured." If this fiend woke up before she got it in a sippy cup, it would go ballistic and trash the shrine to Dead Jim. That would be a drag.

Frantically she rifled through her messenger bag, pulled out a cup and popped off the lid. Picking the unconscious demon up by a foot she carefully dropped it inside the clear plastic container. The lid went on. Then she sank to the floor, the adrenalin fading already.

Now her first solo trapping run had been a success.

Dad is going to be so proud.

The Biblo woke and threw a hellish fit as Riley was completing the paperwork with the hippies in their kitchen. It screamed and banged against the side of the cup like a crazed thing.

"Chill out, will you?" Bandana said. The demon shot him the bird and made a rude remark in Hellspeak.

"What he say?" the man asked.

"Trust me, you don't want to know."

~ - ~ ~

Ten minutes later Riley was headed toward downtown Atlanta, singing along to *Dead and Lovin' It* on the car radio. On the seat next to her was the messenger bag, the signed paperwork and the Offending Minion of Hell. No surprise, it wasn't happy so Riley had learned a couple new fiendish swear words, ones she didn't dare use around her dad. She'd also scored a hug from Sunflower and three strands of beads that didn't go with anything she owned.

What wasn't sitting on the seat next to her was the couple's oversized brownies, though they'd offered to send some home with her. Riley had pleaded a chocolate allergy. It was more like a "I don't need to get busted for weed" issue.

As she edged her way through the intersection onto M.L. King toward downtown Atlanta, the messenger bag began to rock on the seat. She slapped her hand on it to keep it in place while the bag bounced around like a cat with its tail on fire. Tiny feet drummed against her palm as green liquid leaked onto the seat. Somehow the demon had managed to unscrew the sippy cup's lid and now it was a good bet it was trying to find a way out of the bag. If it did, it might take off. What would she tell her dad?

The bag thrashed on the seat and then the demon poked its head out.

"Oh no, you don't! Get back in there." It pulled itself completely free, grinning manically.

Distracted, Riley jerked the steering wheel and nearly collided with another car. The driver honked his horn and glared at her.

"Stop it!" she shouted at the fiend. "You'll get us killed, you idiot."

At the last minute, she looked up and gasped in horror. Ramming her foot on the brake pedal, she plastered herself against the seatbelt causing the messenger bag to careen to the floor. The demon sailed upward and landed on the dash.

There was a screech of burning rubber. "Noooo!"

The car finally halted, missing the one in front of her by inches.

"Thank God," Riley sighed, flopping against the steering wheel in relief. She didn't dare lose her driver's license. It'd taken her two tries to pass the road test.

Peals of demonic laughter came from the dashboard where the demon was doubled over, tears rolling down its eyes in mirth. She made a grab for it, but it skittered out of her reach.

"Hey, I didn't hit him," she said, retrieving her messenger bag from the floor. She had to put the thing back into the cup. The laughter grew louder causing her to hesitate. "What's so funny?"

As she looked up she spied the row of blue lights on top of the car she'd nearly rear-ended. Like you'd see on an emergency vehicle. Or a…

Oh crap.

The Atlanta city cop climbed out of his car and headed her way, a ticket book in hand. His frown promised someone was in deep trouble and that someone was Riley.

"Good thing I passed on the brownies," she murmured.

There was one final burst of hysterical laughter from the demon, then it dove down under the passenger seat, spreading green urine in all directions.

The moment the cop arrived at the car, Riley turned on the charm. She politely handed over her driver's license with green-stained hands and tried to ignore that the car's seats were splattered with demon pee. The smell was worse: rotting gym shoes.

When Riley explained the problem, the cop's right eye began to twitch.

"I've heard 'em all, young lady. Don't even go there."

So she handed over her apprentice license. The cop's frown deepened as he studied it.

"You're kidding me. You're really a trapper?"

"Yes. The demon is under the passenger seat," she said. Or at least she hoped it was. If not, she'd be out one fiend and get a ticket to boot.

Despite her charming personality, the cop wasn't buying her story until she painstakingly fished Hell's smartass from under the seat and dropped it into the sippy cup. She attached the lid with more care this time and then held up the cup so the officer could get a view of the little monster. It promptly flipped him off.

"Oh, God, that's really a … " The guy turned pale and slowly backed away. "You drive safe now," he said and then beat a quick retreat to his car. A few seconds later he sped away, no doubt keen to ticket someone who wasn't packing a demon in their vehicle.

After a lengthy time at a car wash cleaning the seats, the windows and just about everything else inside the vehicle, Riley drove home. When the messenger bag gave another lurch on the seat next to her, she didn't panic: she'd made sure the sippy cup's lid was on tight. From the extent of the demon's swearing, she'd done it right this time.

It hadn't been pretty, but she'd trapped her first Hellspawn on her own.

Her dad was going to be very proud of her.

She cranked up the radio to cover the demon's swearing. Next time she'd get the lid on right. Next time there wouldn't be demon pee all over her and the car.

Next time it'll be perfect.

Author Notes

When I wrote the last sentence in the final Demon Trappers' book, somehow I knew that wasn't going to be the end of Riley and Beck's stories. And not surprisingly, my readers thought the same.

It was only logical to show their time together in Edinburgh during Beck's training. Even though they're a couple, challenges remain. Unfortunately, so does the danger.

It's my hope you enjoyed Grave Matters. Thank you for joining me on Riley and Den's journey.

About the Author

A resident of Atlanta, Georgia, Jana Oliver admits a fascination with all things mysterious, usually laced with a touch of the supernatural. An eclectic person who has traveled the world, she loves to research urban legends and spooky tales.

When not writing, she enjoys Irish music, Cornish fudge and good Scottish whisky.

Find Jana at:
Website: www.JanaOliver.com
Facebook: facebook.com/JanaOliver
Twitter: @CrazyAuthorGirl

Other Books

by Jana Oliver

BRIAR ROSE

Briar Rose believes in fairy tales . . .
And now, because of a family curse, she's living one.

Available in bookstores in the United Kingdom
and Australia and online everywhere else

The Demon Trappers Series

Be sure to check out the rest of the books in this great series by Jana Oliver

U.S. (U.K.) Editions

The Demon Trapper's Daughter (Forsaken)

Soul Thief (Forbidden)

Forgiven

Foretold

34850985R00102

Made in the USA
Lexington, KY
26 August 2014